Out of the Darkness

Untwisted Book Two

D0543569

Out of the Darkness

Untwisted Book Two

Alice Raine

Published by Accent Press Ltd 2015

ISBN 9781783758487

Every man is a moon and has a dark side that he never shows.

Mark Twain

ACKNOWLEDGEMENTS

First and foremost I need to sing the praises of Accent Press and the wonderful people who work there! Without you taking a risk on a new author like me I literally wouldn't be sat here writing acknowledgments for my second published book. Alexandra Davies, my editor and saviour when it comes to all things grammar, thank you for the hours spent pouring over my work. In particular Beth Jones and Stephanie Williams your patience with my endless queries is amazing and I thank you all for the marketing, tweaking, and advice. I know there must also be many more behind the scenes at Accent Press who have worked on my books in one way or another, and although I might not know your names, I send you my deepest gratitude.

Next, a huge thank you to all of my friends who have supported me on this incredible journey! I can't list you all, but you know who you are! A special little mention must go out to Helen L, Karen W, Helen N, Charlotte B, Ruth W, Rosie Mc, Laura Mc, and Katie N, who read, re-read, and provided feedback, advice, and support along the way, not to mention the coffee's, takeaways, and gossip sessions :)

I must thank my husband Paul for the support, love, and encouragement throughout this process, and also my family for their love and pride even though

they knew I didn't want them to read the books!
Your enthusiasm and praise means so much to me.

Now for the really important people … all you lovely
folk reading my books – a huge thank you! I can't
express in words just how much it means to me to
read the great reviews you post, or the fantastic
emails you send me telling me you like my books. To
an author, that is just the best feeling ever, so thank
you, and keep them coming!

The reason I write is for you the reader, so I hope
you enjoy this next instalment.

Alice xx

PROLOGUE

NATHAN

Renewal Form for Club Membership

Club Twist
Explore Your Twisted Side.
101 Fountain Street, Soho, London, W1D 4RF

Name: Nathaniel Jackson
Age: 31
Relationship status: Single
Sexual preference: Women

What do you plan to use our venue for? Please tick at least one box:
☐ Drinking
☐ Socialising
☐ Dancing
■ Meeting sexual partners

When you were younger what influenced the way you viewed sex, relationships and romance (e.g. friends, films, television etc.)?

I've been a member of this club for the last 13 years, but every year I'm made to complete this fucking renewal form. Do you realise how damn insulting that is? I get that you need to assess members for their suitability for a club like the Twist, but the questions on here are ridiculous, especially this one, have you even read it recently? Or considered updating?

Back to the stupid questions. When I was younger I had no best friends – no friends at all actually. I wasn't allowed any. I didn't socialise, it was just one of Father's rules, and I was rarely allowed to watch television, so to put it bluntly, no, friends, films, games or television didn't affect the way I viewed relationships, sex or romance.

The only relationships that have ever mattered to me were those with my father and my brother and both of those are pretty screwed up. And as for romance? It's a fucking waste of time that serves no purpose in my life. Sex I enjoy, but don't kid yourself that sex is in any way linked to romance, it isn't, it's a whole different issue.

Intrinsically men are all arseholes who use women for exactly what they want, I'm just the same – the only difference is I make sure the women I'm with know that all I want is sex to start off with. No blurred lines that way, happy endings all round.

I've answered your fucking questions this time, but next year you either roll my membership over and skip this shit, or you lose me as a member.

STELLA

Application Form for Membership to Club Twist

Club Twist
Explore Your Twisted Side.
101 Fountain Street, Soho, London, W1D 4RF

Name: Stella Marsden
Age: 27
Relationship status: Single
Sexual preference: Men

What do you plan to use our venue for? Please tick at least one box:
■ Drinking
■ Socialising
☐ Dancing
■ Meeting sexual partners

When you were younger what influenced the way you viewed sex, relationships and romance (e.g. friends, films, television etc.)?

Lots of things I suppose. When I was back in my teens my best friend Lilly had been desperately in love with the brooding character of Mr Darcy from *Pride and Prejudice*. We must have watched that bloody series over 20 times but I still remember the day that Lilly announced that she thought all women secretly craved a man who is a bit of a moody bad boy like Darcy. I'd laughed in her face, and in the way that only soppy pre-romance teenagers can, had declared that I would never want a bad boy, only a loving, compassionate, and gentle man like the princes in fairy tales.

It makes me feel old to think about it but quite a few years have passed since that conversation with Lilly, I'm no longer a silly teenager with dreams of fairy tale love, in fact I'm probably rather bitter, having done the relationship thing a few times now, all unsuccessfully, and to be honest rather unsatisfactorily.

It's funny this question is on here, though, because for some reason Lily's words came back to me this afternoon as I sat debating my latest failed romance. After quite a bit of soul-searching and at least half a tub of Ben and Jerry's finest chocolate chip ice cream, I realised that Lilly's statement is quite possibly true for me. I've had gentle and caring boyfriends, but they've lost their appeal pretty quickly, dull, dull and duller ⋯ so I've decided that perhaps it's time I started branching out into brooding bad boy territory too.

That's why I'm here, really; I want to join Club Twist to help me in my search. Even with my decision made I still can't help wondering if the reality of being with a "bad boy" will live up to the fantasy. I suspect not, but I suppose there's only one way to find out – give in this form and then start my search.

ONE – STELLA

Surely this can't be the place? Unconvinced, I glanced along the street again as I approached the blank exterior of what could only be described as an abandoned theatre. A big, boarded-up, empty-looking theatre that had probably seen its heyday back in the seventies. My shoulders sagged – it certainly didn't appear to be a trendy bar and nightclub as I'd been led to believe. Damn, I'd sneaked out of work early and come all this way for a frigging wild goose chase. Sighing, I made the last few steps of my journey anyway and then stopped to glance around the deserted street curiously. I winced, it had a bit of a sleazy feel to it actually; run down, graffiti-covered, and generally just a little bit scummy.

This part of the Soho district of London was totally unknown to me, hell, the whole of Soho was unknown to me. I knew Ronnie Scott's Jazz Club was around here somewhere, and clearly from the sex shops I'd just walked past the local community were somewhat … exuberant in their tastes, shall we say, but that was the sum total of my knowledge.

I myself lived up in Victoria Park, a nice leafy suburb of London that was such a complete contrast to the chewing gum covered pavement where I was currently standing that I had to seriously doubt my sanity for coming here at all. Talk about 'out of your comfort zone'. Mind you, the reason for my visit here today was even crazier, and a little relieved bubble of laughter escaped my throat as I realised that my trip was going to be a dud.

A piece of newspaper blew along the street on the breeze, but even my swift sidestep couldn't stop it from wrapping its greasy pages around my ankle. Just bloody typical. Huffing impatiently, I leant on the theatre wall with a grimace as I tried to shake off the chip wrappings from where it clung to my bare leg. *Ugh*. Finally detaching it I looked up at the broad white columns that lined the old entrance. Frowning, I looked closer. Actually the building wasn't quite as shabby as I'd first believed. From a distance, I'd thought the windows were boarded up, but now I realised that they were covered by discreet but modern shutters.

Narrowing my eyes, I wondered if perhaps I'd been wrong with my first assumption that this theatre had long since seen better days, and as I began to look over the building again I noticed the entrance doors were plain with no markings, but on closer inspection also appeared new and solid.

Standing back a little, I chewed my lower lip nervously as I contemplated the building before me, noticing a discreet logo cast in bronze that was mounted above the set of double doors and glowing a warm amber colour in the afternoon sunshine. I hadn't noticed it on my initial scan of the frontage but it looked like a loose hanging spring, or an apple peel when someone had peeled the entire fruit in one go leaving a long curling piece. It might be simple, but this image told me I had indeed found my destination because it matched the one on the card I clutched in my clammy hand.

Absently fiddling with the ring on my thumb as I did when I was nervous, I glanced down at the slightly crumpled card again. *'Club Twist. Explore your twisted side.'*

One of my eyebrows rose as I read the strap line again. They'd clearly chosen a discreet marketing strategy because the name wasn't exactly specific in its description, but when you turned over the card, the wording and images made it blatantly obvious that Club Twist was a sex club.

Yes, that's right. I, Stella Marsden, professional, independent woman and otherwise sane person, am standing outside the doors to a sex club. I rolled my eyes at my stupid self for ever thinking that this was a good idea. Turning the card in my hand I blushed a prize winning shade of red, apparently Club Twist was no ordinary sex club either, no, they make it their mission to cater for a whole variety of tastes, I know this

6

because there's a frigging list on the reverse of the card that just makes me cringe even reading it.

I now had a big decision to make, after thinking the address had been a dud and that I might have escaped the reason for my trip today I now had to determine if I really wanted to go through with this or not. Did I? *Could I?*

It was now or never. My thumb ring was getting a vigorous twirling as I stood here and considered my options and anxiousness settled so heavily in my belly that I started to feel a bit sick. What was it my flatmate Kenny had told me this morning as he'd seen me off with a bright wave and an encouraging little pep talk ... ah yes, that's right ... "You're a sexually liberated young woman who should go out and get what she damn well wants." Yes, he's all in favour of this crazy plan, but seeing as Kenny is also the sluttiest guy I know I do have to question exactly why it is that I'm following his advice.

After a few more minutes of deliberation, I shrugged and rolled my shoulders in an attempt to relax them. Ah hell, why not, I thought. I can always walk out again can't I? So taking a deep breath I advanced on the large double doors and tentatively gave them a push, surprising myself when I found them unlocked. Taking a shaky breath, I bravely pushed them open, stumbling forwards as their weight gave way and I found myself struggling to see in the darkness within.

'Well hello there,' came a voice through the gloom making me jump out of my frigging skin. Blinking rapidly as my eyes adjusted I calmed myself enough to register that it was indeed a bar inside, and actually it wasn't dingy as I had first thought – merely dimmer than it had been outside in the late afternoon sunshine. The space inside matched the exterior; it was a theatre, or at least it had been at some point before being converted to a bar and nightclub. Crikey, it was cavernous and my inquisitive eyes roved around trying to take it all in while also searching for the source of the voice.

I have to say, it wasn't at all what I had expected of a sex club. There was no leopard print wallpaper, no plastic-covered wipe-clean couches, and not a bed in sight. In fact, there was no obvious sleaziness at all. On the whole, it looked pretty high end, and a whooshing breath of relief flew from my lungs.

My work brain clicked on as I surveyed the room from an interior design perspective. Most of the original features of the theatre seemed to have been maintained, including the huge velvet stage curtains and all the boxes on the upper levels. The only real change seemed to be that the ground floor seats had been removed and replaced with a dance floor and large curved bar with small clusters of tables scattered around the edges. It was surprisingly tasteful and I loved how the original stage had been preserved and neatly joined to the dance floor to form an elevated platform. Whoever had done their interior design had done well, and I felt a vague twinge of envy that it hadn't been my company.

Seeing as the inside looked normal maybe this wouldn't be so bad after all. Blinking back from my thoughts I looked around and realised that the voice I had heard must belong to the lone barman I now saw, who I noticed was unashamedly giving me a very thorough once over before placing down the glass he had been drying.

'H-hi.' My reply was shaky to say the least. The nerves I'd felt as I forced myself to walk through the doors were now completely swamping me and my step faltered before I was even half way across the large room. The cause for my hesitation wasn't just my nerves though, no, a good deal of my sudden anxiousness could definitely be attributed to the feeling of nakedness that swept over my body as the man continued to give me a deep scrutinising look that literally felt like it was stripping me of my clothing, piece by piece. Wow, I'd heard jokes about men who could look through women's clothes with a hot glance, but I'd never experienced it until now. My eyes widened and I swallowed loudly at his inspection, I have to say it was extremely unnerving.

'We're not open yet, sweetheart. Besides, I'm thinking perhaps you're in the wrong place.' The barman continued with a sly smile, sliding his way out from behind the large aluminium covered counter and sauntering towards me. I frowned as his gaze settled happily on my chest so I pulled my jacket protectively around me – not that it would really hide my ample bosoms much – and then stood my ground and raised my chin in an attempt to give myself more confidence. It unfortunately failed, I was still terrified, but hopefully my stance would look convincing to him.

I'd checked the address on the business card practically a dozen times out on the pavement so I knew it was the correct place, but at his words I unnecessarily glanced down at the card in my hand anyway, then frowned and shook my head. 'Nope, this is definitely the right address,' I replied, sounding a little more confident this time as I looked up and met his eyes which had thankfully raised from my cleavage to meet my gaze.

He reached my side and stopped, crossing a thick pair of tattooed arms across his chest. 'Really?' he scoffed, sounding like he didn't believe me for a second. I noticed the smell of alcohol on his breath and dark smudges under his eyes, and wondered if he'd been having a sneaky 'hair of the dog' to help him recover from a big night, or perhaps was just starting early on tonight's session.

'Well, do you want to tell me what a clean-looking little lady like you is doing in my big dirty club then?' he asked in a gravelly tone as his lips turned up in an unnervingly confident smile.

Oh God. I flushed bright red, immediately knowing that his reference to 'dirty' had nothing whatsoever to do with the cleanliness of the club. Even my brief glance earlier had shown it was spotless. No, on this occasion the word was definitely being used in an altogether different context that made me hot under the collar just thinking about it. Was my pursuit of the ultimate 'bad boy' really worth this degree of mortification?

'I'm looking to explore,' I mumbled softly, dying of embarrassment and hoping the barman would understand without making me explain my thoughts in further more humiliating detail.

'Explore? Then you're *definitely* in the wrong place, sweetheart, but there's a stop for a big red tour bus that does the London tourist route just down the road, why don't you try there,' he suggested helpfully while turning me and guiding me back towards the doors with a gentle hand on my back which slipped a bit lower with every step I took.

Realising I was about to be unceremoniously dumped back on the pavement I knew I needed to speak again, and fast. 'Sexually,' I blurted, in what almost sounded like a groan of frustration. 'I want to explore *sexually* ... I was told this was the place to come to.' Ground, please swallow me up. I was cursing bloody Kenny for his stupid suggestion to come here and regretting my even stupider decision to follow up on it.

Stopping just short of the doors with a huge grin spreading across the barman's face I decided it was distinctly possible that he had known all along what I wanted, and had just been playing with me to get his own kicks. *Utter bastard.* Obviously, he liked to make new visitors squirm a little. I grimaced in annoyance, but thankfully managed to keep my sarcastic remarks at bay. After all, I wanted something, and apparently, this man could help me get it.

'Well then, why didn't you just say that in the first place, sweetheart? Looks like you are in the right place after all. Come on in and let's have a chat.' As we walked back towards the bar his hand predictably slipped lower again until he was having a rather good fondle of my bottom. Cheeky sod. Rolling my eyes, I slapped his arm away with a raised eyebrow which made him grin and shrug in a 'can't blame a guy for trying' kind of way. I could have taken his actions as sleazy, but actually he seemed pretty harmless and his playful look made me smile and helped relax my nerves a little.

Once we were seated on tall leather stools, each with a vodka and Coke in front of us, the man finally introduced himself. 'I'm David Halton, the owner of Club Twist, or Dave, whichever you prefer.' Even looking a bit knackered he was fairly attractive in a rough around the edges kind of way, with one of those faces that was difficult to put an age to, tanned and young-looking but with creases on his forehead and at the corners of his eyes which told me he'd lived more years than I initially thought. If the streaks of grey flecking his stubble and the hair at his temples were anything to go by David Halton was probably in his mid-50s, I decided, but his cocksure manner was definitely more suited to a 20-something stud.

'I also own the bar next door for people who want a quieter night, but the entrance is around the corner so you probably missed it.' With another arrogant grin, he held out a hand to me. 'Anyway, back to you, I didn't catch your name, sweetheart.'

I grimaced, that's because I'd deliberately not given it. God this was so out of my comfort zone. What the hell had I been thinking coming here? I was going to kill Kenny tonight, I decided, after I'd made him go out and buy me an entire shelf of chocolate to get me over my humiliation, that was.

Finally deciding that walking through the doors had probably been the hardest part I bit the bullet and answered confidently. 'I'm Stella.' I extended my arm and returned his strong handshake with an equally firm grip of my own. 'I'd prefer to keep it as first names only if that's OK with you.'

In response, David grinned again, a not entirely unattractive sight. 'Not a problem, I'm sure you won't be surprised to know you're not the first visitor to the club who wants to keep their privacy.' He paused and tilted his head thoughtfully. 'In fact, I bet that's not even your real name, is it, sweetheart?'

'It is, actually,' I replied curtly with a small frown as I mentally kicked myself for not using a false name. What an amateur mistake! 'And I'd rather you didn't call me sweetheart,' I added petulantly. Taking a breath, I tried to control myself, my tumbling nerves were making me act with the grace of a fractious 10-year-old, not a woman who was well on her way towards 30.

Luckily, David ignored my little strop. 'So you want to explore sexually. Good on you, too many people these days get caught up in boring relationships and forget to live,' he stated passionately. 'There's so much out there to explore,' he added wistfully. I gave an amused shake of my head. Clearly, this man loved his job, or perhaps his whole lifestyle. 'OK, Stella. Tell me what you're thinking of and I'll tell you if it's something we cater for at my club.'

I felt the blood leave my face as a bout of nerves seemed to briefly stop my heart. Was I really going to have to explain what I wanted out loud and in gory detail? I could hardly just say "I want a bad boy like Mr Darcy" could I? I'd sound completely mental; besides, I actually wanted a bit more than Mr Darcy's level of badness.

Bugger, I'd sort of hoped there might be a questionnaire to fill in, or at the very least a tick box list I could use … anything that would have allowed me to avoid stating my sexual preferences out loud in front of a complete stranger. A complete stranger who was grinning as if thoroughly enjoying every second of my discomfort. Narrowing my eyes at him, I confirmed my earlier beliefs. He *was* definitely an utter bastard.

Picking up on my hesitancy David finally spoke again. 'It's fine to be nervous, sweetheart,' he started, ignoring my earlier request not to call me by the nickname. 'Let me tell you what we offer here at Club Twist and you see if anything sounds good.'

Releasing a breath of relief, I nodded gratefully and decided that after his thoughtful gesture I was willing to give David Halton another chance, maybe he wasn't so bad after all.

'So basically we're a sex club, you can come here for a drink, a partner, or just to watch our shows. As such we make sure most preferences are catered for, if you're interested in sex with strangers, bondage, domination, voyeurism, multiple partners, or girl on girl action then we can help you out.' I'd read as much on the business card, but hearing it brashly stated out loud had caused my eyes to widen like saucers Wow, it was a veritable menu of sexual deviancy, and apparently I was at the buffet.

David sat back looking so proud of his business that I very nearly laughed out loud. 'Or if there's something even more specific you're after I can probably find someone to accommodate your preferences,' he added. Then, after a lengthy pause, David raised his eyebrows expectantly obviously hoping for a response from me.

'Well … I …' I paused nervously again, since my break-up from my ex, Aidan, I'd spent months considering the direction of my life and had decided focusing on my career was the path I wanted to go down for the time being. But I was a woman, I had certain needs … needs that Aidan had brought to the surface … God, why was it so hard to say out loud? 'My last

12

partner introduced me to the idea of domination ...' I finally said weakly. 'I'd like to explore that some more.' Yep, after several vodkas last night, I'd decided that a dominant guy would surely be the ultimate bad boy. Wouldn't he? Well hell, if I was going to do this I wanted to do it properly.

'OK, and in this relationship were you the dominant partner or the submissive one?' David asked without so much as pausing for breath or blinking an eye. I snorted an embarrassed breath as I briefly wondered how many times in his life David had asked that very same question and almost giggled hysterically, what completely different circles we travelled in!

'Submissive,' I whispered, twirling my thumb ring frantically and still unable to believe I was voicing these things out loud to a complete stranger.

'Really?' David seemed genuinely surprised. 'With your temperament so far I'd have had you down as the one in charge,' he said with a wiggle of his eyebrows. 'I hope you don't mind but I need to ask why you're not still with your ex.'

'We just wanted different things,' I said vaguely, not wanting to explain that while I'd enjoyed being in the bedroom with Aidan, he had been as dull as dishwater outside of the sheets. Once he'd started to hint at getting engaged, I'd made a speedy exit from the relationship. 'But I enjoyed the domination stuff ... I'd like to try it with someone who's a bit more experienced.'

Nodding David took another hearty swig of his drink before smiling at me broadly. 'I'm sure that can be arranged, sweetheart.'

'Another thing,' I added quickly, 'I know from research that there are various different types of dom/sub relationships and I was kind of hoping for a fairly "no strings attached" set up.' Seeing David's inquisitive glance I swallowed and elaborated. 'I have a really stressful job, my focus is on my career for now, but I think this could be a perfect way to release some of the control I use all day, I want to settle down and have kids eventually but not yet, there's too much going on at work so I'm not looking for a long-term commitment, maybe just six months or so to start with.'

David's eyes lit up at my statement. 'I think I may just know the perfect guy,' he said standing up and heading behind the bar in search of something before pausing and lifting his head with a frown. 'That is assuming you want a male partner?'

Losing count of how many times I had flushed red in the last ten minutes I nodded sharply to which David smiled and continued with his search below the counter. 'Great, the guy I'm thinking of is an experienced dom with a very good reputation, plus they don't come more "strings-free" than Nathan. He's not been into the bar for ages so let me see if he's involved with anyone at the moment. You can fill in a quick membership form while I call him.'

David reappeared clutching an address book that he had obviously been searching for. Sliding a membership form across the bar to me, he flashed me a smile before dialling a number and disappearing to make his call leaving me sat nibbling on my lip and feeling slightly detached from the whole weird situation I'd managed to get myself into.

TWO – NATHAN

I frowned and ran a hand though my blond hair. It was a touch longer than I liked and needed a cut really, but that wasn't my main issue tonight. The thing that was really bugging me was that I wasn't entirely sure why I was pulling into the car park of Club Twist and that fact bothered me a great deal.

I was the master of my life, I controlled everything, planned every single little detail, and going out for a drink definitely had *not* been within my plans for the evening.

Once again, I asked myself what the fuck I was doing here but still found no suitable answer. Yes, I was currently unattached, but that was the way I'd wanted things; business was too brisk to bother with the shit that comes with personal relationships, and yet even with that fact in the forefront of my mind I still found myself here climbing from my car after the call from David Halton a few hours ago. In fact when I'd got the call from my old associate saying there was a submissive in the club looking for a new partner I'd actually stood straight up and headed immediately for a shower.

Pathetic. I made a low noise of disgust in the back of my throat. I should just turn the car around and go home, I didn't need a submissive at the moment, and I sure as hell didn't want David having a reason to be all smug around me and thinking that I owed him a favour.

Even as this last thought left my brain, I still found myself climbing from my car. *What the hell was wrong with me?* I wondered idly, as I locked my BMW, straightened my navy suit jacket and headed across the tarmac to the club's back entrance. Did I just need to get laid perhaps? It had been a while since I'd had sex after all. Or maybe it was just curiosity, David had said the woman was a stunner but seemed innocent too, a combination that had instantly appealed to me. Nodding decisively I headed towards the back door of the club. Yes, that was probably it, I'd see her to ease my curiosity and then return to my well-ordered life. I could always call one of the many women in my address book for a quick fuck midweek to clear my mind if need be.

As if sensing my arrival I was practically knocked backwards by the overzealous welcome of David Halton. This guy was such an over the top dick. His beefy arms wrapped around me as if we were best fucking buddies and I suddenly found myself surrounded by his unwelcome smell which was predominantly tobacco, but with an underlying odour of stale mint and sweat mixed in. Jesus, he had no clue about the etiquette of personal space. Or personal hygiene for that matter.

Grimacing over his shoulder, I managed to disengage him from my body, and then stepped away and brushed my hands down my jacket to smooth it. Loosening off my neck, I counted down from five in my head to calm myself and then attempted a small tight smile.

Now at a safe distance, I looked over at my old friend who was chattering away at me, although being a sleazy womaniser David Halton wasn't really a friend of mine as such, more of an acquaintance. An acquaintance that I always seemed to end up wanting to punch after a few minutes spent together, because as well as some serious issues with being way too tactile for a straight guy, he also never knew when to shut the hell up.

After knowing him for as long as I had, David really should know two key things about me by now: Firstly, I don't do physical contact with someone unless I plan on fucking them, and secondly, I'm a quiet guy, I like my silence and can't tolerate incessant babble for the sake of it.

In truth, I'd known David Halton since the day I'd stumbled into Club Twist as a confused teenager hoping that the people inside would be able to reassure me that the fact that I liked to control every aspect of my life, women included, wasn't an abnormal trait. Yeah, obsessive-compulsive disorder doesn't even go half way to describing my issues. To be honest,

David's immediate acceptance of me back then was the only thing that had stopped me hitting the arrogant arsehole over the years that had since passed.

My dislike of David was mostly due to the man's insatiable promiscuity and complete disregard for his lovers. I was no hearts and flowers man, but the women I slept with were always clearly told up front what to expect with me – sex, and sex only, nothing more. David on the other hand would promise, lie, and cajole his way into a woman's knickers and not feel an ounce of guilt the following morning when he walked out their door promising to call when he so clearly never would.

I might not like the guy, but right now, I couldn't help but feel a grudging thankfulness towards him as my eyes settled on the woman that David was now pointing out to me across the bar.

'So I figured no one I know is more "no strings attached" than you, mate.' He had that part right, commitments of the romantic type I *did not* do. Ever.

'And you've got to agree she's pretty hot, isn't she?' David bragged proudly, to which I merely grunted in response, my attention now too captivated by the woman at the bar to answer David's questions. 'If I wasn't already set up to screw that Russian bird and her sister tonight I would have been tempted to take her home myself and teach her a thing or two about domination, if you know what I mean!' David leered making my lips curl in annoyance as the urge to finally give in and punch him increased by several notches.

'Come on, I'll introduce you.' David offered, stepping around a table in the direction of the bar.

Not a chance, I wasn't giving David even the remotest opportunity to make a move on this woman – she was mine. *Fuck*, where the hell had that thought come from? I'd not even spoken to her yet, but apparently, my body was intent on ownership. *Calm down,* I briefly closed my eyes and took a breath to steady myself, then reached out a hand to stop David by trapping his wrist in a firm grip before finally finding my voice. 'No, thank you, David; I'll be fine from here.' The last thing I wanted was David's non-stop drivel to put the poor woman off. I'd be far better off introducing myself.

Once David had got the hint and reluctantly returned to work, I let my gaze wander back to the woman at the bar. Just one glance at her made me believe that David was a master of the understatement because she wasn't stunning, as he had said, she was beautiful. Completely beautiful in a natural, innocent, and no doubt highly addictive way. No shovelled-on make-up or fake breasts here, no, she looked one hundred per cent real, and one hundred per cent delectably fuckable.

A strange feeling passed through my chest and as well as feeling slightly breathless I also found that I couldn't seem to take my eyes off her. My cock also noted its approval by giving a little twitch in my boxers and I scowled, hating my uncharacteristic loss of control. I instantly made a mental note not to go so long without sex in future.

It was difficult to guess her height because of the bar stool she was sitting on, but it did nothing to disguise the trim legs that flowed out from a fitted skirt and hung down to her delicate ankles and expensive high heels. I do love a woman in a good pair of heels, preferably naked and standing in my bedroom expectantly, or perhaps with just the addition of some shackles or suspenders. Blinking away my fantasy, I took note of her fine, long, blonde hair that flowed around her pretty face to her shoulders and curled attractively over what seemed to be an ample chest. All in all, she appeared to be a most tempting package and I was suddenly glad that I'd made the effort to come down to the bar tonight after all.

Once my raging libido calmed I saw past her looks and noticed that her posture radiated nervous discomfort, was she apprehensive about meeting me, I wondered briefly. She probably should be; a lovely thing like her should never get mixed up with damaged goods like me. But seeing her eyes dart to her left, widen, and then quickly return to her drink I smiled. Clearly, she wasn't a regular patron of the Twist because it was the sexual dance that the two young men were performing on the pedestal to her left that appeared to be the cause of her discomfort, not her imminent meeting with me. *Christ*, her posture was immaculate. In fact she was currently sat in a

18

position that I was finding quite appealing; submissive, sexy, and shy all at once.

Just about fucking perfect as far as I was concerned.

A dry laugh escaped my throat as I continued to watch her discomfort over the dancers, embarrassed by a fairly tame dance routine, was she? I smiled again at how innocent she seemed, sat there surrounded by a whole range of people from London's most deviant community. She was like an angel fluttering helplessly in room packed full of demons.

As much as I knew I should walk away from an innocent like her I couldn't help myself, I'd always loved the idea of breaking in a newbie. This could be even more fun than I'd first anticipated.

Deciding that I was selfish enough to want her even though my tastes would probably be too demanding for her I straightened my suit and ran a hand across my hair to smooth it. I'd had enough of simply looking at her, and began to stride confidently across the bar towards the blonde, stopping just short of her bar stool before crossing my arms as I waited for her to notice me. She could make the first move. Well, I might as well start off as I mean to go on.

THREE – STELLA

Oh God, oh God, oh God, about ten seconds ago I had noticed a man approaching me in my peripheral vision, but when he'd stopped right next to me I had been too nervous to bring myself to turn and face him and had stared fixedly at my drink instead. Now I was still sat staring at the slice of lemon in my vodka and probably looked like a complete frigging idiot. Great; good start, Stella. Sucking in a huge breath I readied myself. This was it, I'd come here wanting to enter a relationship as a submissive and now, stood waiting for me to acknowledge him was my potential dom. My ultimate bad boy.

I'd quite literally never felt more anxious in my entire life. Scared shitless doesn't even come close.

There really was only so long that you could stare at a slice of lemon without being carted off to a loony bin, so finally I shifted in my seat and nervously turned to face the man silently assessing me.

My heart was absolutely pounding in my chest but I'd promised myself that I would use my business head and remain cool, calm, and collected in this meeting. Unfortunately as I took my first cautious glance at the man to my right those promises became a thing of the past.

Blimey. Without even speaking, he had instantly managed to make me feel intimidated. He was well over six feet tall, but the first thing I noticed about him was that he had the clearest, brightest, most icily intense blue eyes I'd ever seen. They were so cold-looking that my heart stuttered and I actually found myself shivering. To match his impressive height he was classically good-looking, handsome even, and seemed to have a great build to match: broad and athletic, which was made more pronounced by the impeccably tailored suit that clung to him tantalisingly. All this was topped off with a mop of shockingly blond hair swept back with precision from his forehead. My mouth dropped open in astonishment and it took a great deal of mental effort to close it again.

I have to say I'd never really gone for blonds before, but for this man I'd happily change my preference because, quite simply, he was stunning.

All in all he screamed authority, professionalism, and a raw masculine sex appeal that made my poor pounding heart quiver in my chest with apprehension.

Now that I was finally looking at him I found he dropped his eyes to focus them somewhere around my chin before giving me a curt nod and sitting himself on the stool next to me. I frowned and wondered why he had averted his eyes, but the only reason I could come up with was that perhaps he was trying to make me feel more comfortable by not staring at me directly. Perhaps he knew the heart stopping effect that his piercing blue eyes had and found it easier to converse this way. Whatever the reason it was fast becoming clear to me that I had never before had a reaction to a man like this.

'You must be Stella, I'm Nathan,' he said in a deep, rich voice that matched his impressive stature and did nothing to calm my thundering heart.

In response, I nodded and realised that my nervy dry throat had completely removed my ability to speak. This man, *Nathan*, literally radiated presence. One that not many people had or could pull off; a mixture of arrogance, self-confidence, and sheer masculine intensity that sent an involuntary shudder of fear laced lust bursting through my body. My God, I was desperately turned on already and he'd only said six words to me!

Undoubtedly, Nathan must be the kind of man that drew looks of admiration when he entered a room. Women would want to be with him and men would want to be like him. From my admittedly limited experience he was a rarity, some sort of prime specimen of masculinity that up until now I had thought only existed in magazines or cheesy action flicks. I swallowed nervously as I considered him, there was no doubt that he was way out of my league and without even saying one word to him I already sensed that I was probably in over my head with this guy.

'So, David tells me you might be looking for a new partnership with a dominant,' Nathan stated calmly, obviously not feeling any of the nerves or embarrassment that were currently coursing through my veins like a freight train.

Quickly sipping my drink to quench my parched throat I finally managed to speak. 'Um, yes.' Fiddling with my glass I decided I needed to be completely upfront with this guy from the start. 'I should warn you I'm not hugely experienced in this type of relationship,' – major understatement – 'but I know it's definitely something I'd like to experiment with.'

'Yes, David explained some of your history to me on the phone,' Nathan replied coolly. 'He said your career is your main focus at the moment, but that after a failed relationship with a different dominant you are now interested in pursuing a purely physical relationship with someone else.' Tilting his head, he swirled his glass, as if considering the possible reasons that my relationship 'failed', a tiny flicker of a smile moving his lips. His very lovely lips, I realised distractedly, as my eyes lingered on them for just a little longer than necessary.

Feeling a little defensive of myself, I straightened my back. 'We just wanted different things,' I clarified haughtily.

'Quite frankly, if you had a contractual agreement I have no idea how your "differences" didn't come up as an issue at the start of your relationship,' Nathan said with a shake of his head.

'It wasn't really a contractual thing, we met through a friend and he only admitted he was into the dominant stuff later on,' I observed. Picking up on the minute shake of Nathan's head, I assumed it was because he thought me stupid for not having had some sort of contract with Aidan.

Nathan's condescending remark made me feel decidedly prickly about my naivety, and I sat up straighter on my stool to defend myself. 'You need to understand I've never had a relationship before that required a contract,' I reminded him, wanting to sound clear and confident and brisk, but unfortunately my words came out weakly as I once again realised how ridiculously out of my depth I was. Talk about throwing yourself in the deep end! Maybe I should just leave now. For one thing, I'd never really been in a submissive relationship before, but on top of that I'd never so much as kissed a man as startlingly attractive and commanding as the one currently sat in front of me and that thought completely frigging terrified me.

'Of course,' Nathan conceded finally, 'I appreciate it's a different approach from the norm. I, however, would expect a contract to be drawn up between us, it would ensure we both achieved satisfaction from the agreement while also staying within both of our boundaries,' he stated clearly.

'I'll be upfront with you, I'm concerned that as a relative novice to this world my tastes may be a little extreme for you,' he said with a frown, still avoiding eye contact with me by focusing his attention on straightening his shirt cuffs.

Extreme? My blush paled from my cheeks as my mind flashed to some of the more disturbing images I'd seen when looking up Club Twist on the internet, it might make me uncomfortable to ask him, but this was something I needed to broach right away. 'Um … OK … what exactly is it you like to do?' I asked nervously.

With an unembarrassed shrug, Nathan began to explain, 'I have to lead, I demand complete control and submission, often using bondage. I can be rough –' he added, glancing briefly at me '– and I will administer punishments if my wishes are not followed. I will push you to your limits, Stella, but never against your will.' I swallowed hard and put my glass down before my trembling hand dropped it. Blimey, was it suddenly warmer in here?

Rough wouldn't be a problem, truth be told. Aidan was the only partner I'd had who liked it rough and after being with him I'd realised that I did too, but pushing me to my limits? What the hell did he mean by that? But before I could ask, Nathan met my gaze briefly with his hard blue eyes and continued, 'I'm not looking for a girlfriend or romance, this would simply be a mutually beneficial agreement between two adults who are looking for some sexual release.'

I blushed wildly at his brisk assessment of our situation – "adults needing sexual release" – but at least he was being honest and upfront with me. 'That sounds ... fine.' Actually, it was pretty much what I'd assumed most dominants did, and exactly what I was looking for. My career was my priority at the moment.

'So what I'm suggesting sounds suitable for your tastes?' Nathan sounded dubious which for some reason I found quite amusing and a small smile slipped to my lips.

'Yes, like you mentioned earlier, I currently have a job with quite a lot of responsibility so I don't have time for a standard relationship either. I'm not embarrassed to admit that I like sex though,' Pushing back my shoulders I straightened my spine hoping I didn't look as out of my depth as I felt, 'Seeing as I'm looking for an outlet for my stress, a distraction if you like, I thought that handing over control sexually could be a good solution. That way I get to enjoy myself physically but won't have to think about decisions until I go back to work the following week.'

Once again Nathan's eyes briefly flicked to mine and I watched as his eyebrows rose at my honest response, but after his initial shock, his lips twitched. Apparently he was pleased with my words. 'And the bondage? You don't mind being tied up? Controlled? Punished even?' he asked, running his finger around the rim of his glass, which I suspected was a further way to avoid looking me in the eye. He certainly avoided eye contact a lot, there seemed to be an issue there. Perhaps when I felt braver with him I'd ask him about it.

'We'd need to discuss some limits, but like I said, I'm looking for a distraction from my stress. I think what you're suggesting could be quite distracting,' I added feeling ridiculously shy, once again my eyes averted in embarrassment and I felt my cheeks blush for what felt like the thousandth time today. Thank God I'd opted for minimal make-up and wasn't wearing blusher too.

'I think there is potential for a mutually beneficial agreement here, Stella,' Nathan concluded firmly, and my heart accelerated in my chest forcefully. 'I would, however, need your assurance that this would stay discreetly between us. You may not recognise me but I'm fairly well known in the business sector of London so it is imperative to me that my lifestyle choices remain private.'

Thank goodness. 'Indeed, privacy goes without saying,' I agreed quickly. 'I also want complete privacy in this agreement. I will only be telling my best friend, and I'd rather that no one outside of your most trusted friends know what I do in my free time.' God, I couldn't even begin to imagine the chaos that would erupt in my office if my employees found out, let alone my family. A shiver ran through me at the image of my father screaming bloody murder and my mother in a full dramatic faint on the floor, gosh, just thinking about it made me cringe.

'Good. In that case, can we swap full names now? I'm Nathaniel Jackson, but I prefer Nathan,' he said holding out a hand out to me.

My heart practically stopped in my chest at his words and I couldn't help the widening of my eyes. *Nathaniel Jackson?* Had I heard him correctly? 'As in NJA? Nathaniel Jackson Architecture?' I asked in a shocked whisper, causing him to break his apparent 'no eye contact' rule and meet my gaze with a narrowed glance that conveyed obvious concern.

'Clearly you are familiar with my company,' he stated in an icy tone as he dropped his extended hand firmly back on his thigh. Oops, perhaps he hadn't liked my reaction.

Blinking in surprise at this unexpected turn of events I almost laughed out loud from nerves. 'Y-yes, I'm an interior designer for Markis Interiors, we do out most of the interiors of the buildings that NJA design and build.' My tone was questioning, would someone as important as the CEO actually know the names of his lowly contractors?

To his credit, Nathan looked as shocked as I had been. 'Markis? Of course, they're our main contractor. What a small world.' Pausing, he tilted his head considering me with narrowed eyes. 'Will this be an issue?' The tone of his words was almost threatening but I tried to ignore them, after all I was hardly going to blab in the office about him being a sexual dominant was I? That would merely bring up questions as to how I knew about his sex life and imply that I knew him intimately ... a topic I certainly wasn't planning on discussing in the next team meeting.

'I don't see why it should be, it's not like we've ever met through work before,' I decided with a shrug that I hoped looked casual. In fact, thinking about it, I didn't think that Nathan had ever graced the Markis offices with a personal visit, normally the lead designers were simply summoned to his offices when a contract was won. I would certainly remember meeting a man as stunning as Nathan; that was for sure. Suddenly it hit me how crazy this all was ... I was sat in a bar making plans to be a sexual submissive for the boss of the company that kept me in work!

'Agreed,' he said, clearly not feeling the nerves I was. 'Your full name, then?' he prompted again, apparently not liking the imbalance of personal details we had shared till now.

'Stella Marsden,' I mumbled softly. It was done now: he knew who I was and where I worked and there was no taking it back. Then again, I knew who he was too, and that was clearly someone who was much more important and well known than me.

God, he was the owner and managing director of the most famed architectural consultants in London, for goodness sake. Even though he was still young, just 31, he was renowned for slashing prices by providing a full design and build service, effectively cutting out the builder costs and so dropping the overall price of jobs. NJA literally accounted for eighty per cent of the business my office dealt with. And I was planning on sleeping with him. Rolling my eyes I shook my head at how crazy this was. How did I always manage to get myself into trouble like this?

Marginally adjusting what appeared to be an already perfect tie Nathan finished his drink and then changed the topic entirely. 'Would you consent to having some tests done? ' he asked bluntly without any further explanation.

Tests? Obviously seeing my frown, Nathan expanded on his point. 'I would like to ensure there is no risk of sexually transmitted diseases being passed between us; taking some simple STD tests is standard for me with a new partner. Also, if we do decide to proceed and you were to agree to use a form of contraception like the pill we could forego condoms if you were happy to.'

Right, of course. I'd been so nervous meeting him I hadn't even considered the issue of STDs. Just another show of my complete naive stupidity. 'I assume you will take the tests too so I know I'm also safe?' I questioned in a challenging tone, which he met with an imperious look. Cringing slightly, I suspected that a good submissive would have merely agreed immediately rather than challenge their new dominant. Oops, my first blunder. I suspected there would be many to follow.

'I'm tested regularly, but yes, if it will make you happy I will also have them done,' he conceded with a narrowed gaze directed at my chin. Score one for me, I allowed myself a small smile at this tiny victory.

'Perhaps we could meet tomorrow evening to discuss further details, maybe somewhere a little more private,' he said glancing around the busy interior of the club which was now getting rather full.

'OK. By the way, with regards to your other point I already have the contraceptive injection,' I explained softly, no doubt looking embarrassed once again. Add it to the list; I was used to my burning cheeks by now.

'Are you good at remembering to get it done?' Nathan asked curtly, and from the look on his face I suspected that a pregnant submissive was the last thing he wanted to be dealing with.

'Not really,' I replied with a small smile, at work I was an ordered machine but at home – hideously disorganised. 'But I pay my doctors a fee for a special reminder service. They call me non-stop in the three weeks before it's due.'

Nodding his satisfaction Nathan slipped from his chair. 'Good. Shall we get those tests done now? The club is very up on its hygiene so it has its own clinic attached. They'll be able to process them overnight.'

'Sure.' And just like that, it was done. Nathan and I headed towards the clinic next door and agreed to meet the following evening in the privacy of his apartment to discuss further details. Privacy was good, I decided, less people to overhear and less chance of seeing someone I recognised, but as I trailed after the domineering figure of Nathaniel Jackson it suddenly occurred to me that privacy would also mean being in the same room, alone with all his masculine intensity. *Crikey*. My eyes widened as panic began to set in. Was I really going to have sex with that man? That God-like figure who was causing every woman in the place to stare?

Luckily, my panic was quickly replaced by my irrational fear of doctors as we reached the tiny clinic and were ushered inside.

FOUR - NATHAN

After returning home from the club I dumped my car keys on the kitchen counter and headed straight to the lounge bar where I poured myself a large whiskey, deciding that tonight only the finest single malt would do. Downing the first shot in one go I refilled the glass and then rolled my shoulders, trying to relieve the tension I was carrying.

After depositing my whisky on the coffee table I flopped back onto a sofa, then scowled at myself and sat up straighter. Control over everything was vital to me, *everything*, right down to the state of my posture, and that small slip of 'flopping on the sofa' just showed exactly how much Stella Marsden had already got under my skin. I didn't like this realisation, not one bit.

I was seriously keyed up after my meeting with Stella, but that wasn't the only reason that my mind was in overdrive; returning to Club Twist for the first time in many months had prompted long-buried thoughts to return to my mind. It wasn't often that I allowed my mind to slip back to childhood memories, I had good reason to deliberately avoid it, but for some reason tonight's occurrences with the naïve Stella had sent my mind tumbling back to where it had all started, the very reason that control had become so important to me.

Closing my eyes I set my head back on the sofa and begrudgingly allowed the plush luxury of my hard-earned London penthouse to melt away, and be replaced in my mind's eye by the tatty, pale yellow walls of my childhood bedroom. God I had hated that crappy wallpaper …

Suddenly I was ten years old again and my father was leaning over me, muttering under his breath about what selfish, ignorant children he had fathered. If I looked up I knew that my father's eyes would be bloodshot and enraged and that the weird lumpy vein on his temple would be pulsating wildly like it was about to burst.

But I didn't look up.

I'd learnt many years ago as a young boy that I never looked Father in the eye. *Never*.

Not unless I wanted the beating of a lifetime that would bruise my behind so badly that it would stop me riding my bike in the garden for at least a week. Riding my bike within the garden fences was the only time I was allowed to leave the confines of the house, and as such, it was precious to me and not something to be toyed with.

Don't look up.

Thinking about it, I couldn't actually remember the last time I'd looked anyone directly in the eye. Not my father, mother, teachers, or even the boys in my class. It simply wasn't allowed at home so I'd extended the habit to all areas of my life. Not that the boys at school mattered, they all thought I was a freak anyway and avoided me like a plague victim.

The exception to the rule was my little brother Nicholas. I often looked Nicholas in the eye when I was trying to calm him down and stop him crying after one of Father's beatings. Which was basically every evening in those days. For whatever reason poor Nicholas always seemed to get it worse than I did, but while I was powerless to stop my father's onslaughts I made it my duty to be there to pick Nicholas up afterwards.

Clenching my teeth, I watched as my father unbuckled his belt and slid it from the loops of his trousers. I didn't need to ask what was coming next, that much was obvious, all I could do was thank my lucky stars that father was wearing the broad brown belt today and not the narrow black one. The black one hurt so much more.

The black one was usually saved for Nicholas.

I would beg my father to use the black belt on me instead of my younger brother, but my requests were always met with derision. 'That boy needs discipline more than you. You understand that I'm doing this for your own good to help you understand the world. Nicholas just screams like a big baby and lashes out at me. Biggest fucking mistake of my life, that kid. Needs a fucking cane, not just a belt,' my father often muttered.

Somehow, over the many years that I endured the beatings I came to believe some of what my father said, not the things about Nicholas being bad, I would never believe anything bad about my baby brother, but the words about myself. Maybe I did need to be taught right from wrong; maybe my father was simply doing this for my own good. I learnt to respect the relationship with my father, and I suppose I almost regarded the older man with a reverent respect for how he controlled everything within the sphere of our home.

He controlled everything. I wanted to be like that.

FIVE – STELLA

An insatiable bout of nerves kicked in to my stomach at approximately 1.37 p.m. the following day when my phone rang and I received the results of my tests. Up until this point, I had managed to forget about that evening's planned meeting with the sexy Adonis that was Nathaniel Jackson. Well, not forget so much, but push it to the back of my mind so I could at least pretend to be a normally functioning human and do something productive with my day.

The nurse was very sweet on the phone, patiently explaining everything, and as expected I got an all clear. Once I had hung up my heart began to hammer in my chest, something which seemed to be happening quite a lot lately.

It was really happening. Tonight I was meeting Nathaniel Jackson, my proposed dominant, also known as my 'bad boy incarnate', in the privacy of his apartment. Who knew what might happen …

'Oh my God!' came a shrill shriek from down the corridor, interrupting the start of my fantasy. 'Was that him calling? Was it? I wanted you to put him on speaker phone so I could hear the sexy voice you were telling me about!' Kenny, my flatmate, came dashing into the lounge flushed from the exertion of running down the three-foot long corridor, and then skidded to a halt by me as he doubled over to catch his breath in a style that was typically dramatic, and typically Kenny. God, he was such a drama queen.

'No, it was just my test results coming through. He's not going to call me, we've already arranged the details for tonight,' I explained in a tone that was far calmer than I felt.

'True,' Kenny agreed, standing upright again and suddenly

looking no worse off for his run. 'You can't disapprove of my enthusiasm, Stella, my love life's so dull that I'm living vicariously through you, sweetie,' he said with a dimpled grin that made his goatee beard wiggle.

I raised my eyebrows at him. Since we had started sharing a flat together two years ago Kenny had been through more men than I could ever count; his love life was *anything* but dull.

My eyebrows rose even higher as I watched him grab a bottle of brown liquid from the kitchen counter and swig from it.

'Ugh, Kenny, what the hell is that?' I asked, wincing at the disgusting gunk in the bottle that closely resembled something I'd dredged up from the bottom of a pond when studying geography at school.

'I'm on a new liquid diet, vegetable smoothies only,' he informed me primly. 'This one is parsnip, beetroot, and ...' His eyes went to the ceiling as he tried to recall the ingredients. 'I can't remember, but apparently it's very good for speeding up my metabolism and increasing weight loss,' he informed me airily taking another swig then holding the drink out to me.

Grimacing, I gingerly sniffed the bottle before gagging. Ugh, forget pond bottoms, it smelt like something you might find decomposing in a long lost rubbish bin. Kenny was always on some new fad diet, not that he needed to lose weight, but the contents of that bottle smelt truly grim. 'And it's good?' I enquired warily.

'Nah, tastes like crap,' Kenny said dismissively, making me snort with laughter. 'Anyway, stop trying to change the subject away from lover boy, I still can't believe you didn't get a picture of him to show me,' he grumbled with a pout, tilting his hip out and resting on the kitchen counter.

'Yeah, and exactly how would I have managed that, Kenny?' I asked with a grin, trying to imagine pulling out a camera and asking Nathan – Mr Intense and Moody – to 'say cheese' for a picture.

'By telling him that your gay flat mate needs to check him out and make sure he's hot enough for you before you bed him,' Kenny replied swiftly with a challenging lift of his brow.

Bed him. *Oh God,* I was going to be bedding Nathaniel Jackson at some point in the very near future. The thought suddenly hit me with such force that I felt quite light headed and had to grab onto Kenny for support as my legs went rubbery below me.

'Woah! Easy, girl!' he said, holding me up and leading me over to one of the stools before fetching me a glass of water with a worried expression on his face.

'God, I can't believe I'm doing this,' I murmured, placing my head into my hands to try and steady my spinning brain. My stomach suddenly felt like it was promptly going to rid itself of my sushi lunch and I was fairly sure that I was now sweating profusely.

Turning to Kenny I punched him in the arm, hard. 'More to the point, I can't believe you bloody well talked me into it!' I mean seriously, what kind of friend persuades their mate to go to a sex club and pick up a dominant? One look at Kenny and his outrageously tight jeans and small pink waistcoat gave me my answer. A friend with absolutely no morals when it came to sex; a friend just like Kenny.

Taking several deep breaths I calmed myself enough to clear the dizzy spell that was rushing through my head and my sushi thankfully stayed intact. Ugh, raw fish floating in the toilet bowl would not have been a good start to the afternoon.

Glancing at the kitchen clock, I noted that I had about five hours left before my meeting with Nathan. Just five hours. No doubt they would pass in the blink of an eye given my current state of agitation.

I was getting myself worked up over nothing – tonight was simply a meeting to discuss the terms of our proposed agreement, so no sexual interactions would be happening, would they? Allowing my eyes to close for a second I briefly indulged in a few moments fantasising about just how exhilarating intimate situations with a man as overtly masculine as Nathan would be. Very exhilarating, I bet. Gosh, it had been a while since I'd been to bed with a man, let alone one as sexy as Nathan, and an involuntary shudder of desire ran through me at the thought.

Kenny must have seen my little quiver because his grin widened and I flushed as bright red as the Comic Relief nose stuck to the fridge door. I needed to distract myself, and Kenny, who was now giving me and my blush a rather odd look, so I dragged him into my bedroom to plan my outfit in advance. Once my clothing choices were settled – black skirt, silk blouse, and knee-high boots – Kenny also persuaded me to call my beauty salon for an emergency leg, underarm, and bikini wax even though I repeatedly insisted I wouldn't be having sex tonight.

'Think like a boy scout,' Kenny said with a smirk, but his random statement totally confused me. What the hell did scouts have to do with leg waxes? Seeing my puzzled expression, Kenny chuckled. 'Always be prepared!' he said with a wink as he pushed me out the door towards the beauticians.

SIX – NATHAN

I was pacing my apartment so impatiently that I had practically cut a track in the carpet by my fireplace. My personally sourced and very expensive Italian carpet, which probably deserved far better treatment. I grimaced and on a growl moved my pacing area towards the more durable wooden flooring near the windows instead.

Stella wasn't late for our meeting, but for the last two hours I'd felt like a caged tiger. I'd deliberately opted to be without a submissive for nearly six months now, but the anticipation of my upcoming meeting with the inexperienced Stella was literally driving me to distraction with the possibilities it presented. The possibilities *she* presented.

When the doorbell finally rang, I had to resist the temptation to rush across the lounge and rip the fucking thing from its hinges. Instead I paused by the fireplace, gripped the mantle, and repeated my personal mantra in my head to help me reign in my faltering control that was usually so rigidly in place. *No one can control me. I am in ultimate control.*

Feeling calmer now, I donned my impenetrable front once again and opened the door, briefly allowing myself to meet Stella's wide but confident blue gaze for the sake of politeness. I would have to explain my issue with eye contact at some point this evening, otherwise she was bound to notice and question me on it and I really fucking hated it when people did that. Mind you, most people were too intimidated by me to question it these days; perhaps Stella would be the same.

A smirk curved my lip as I ran my gaze down her appearance. I decided that my memories of Stella from last night hadn't done her justice, nowhere close – even with her hair pinned up and just the barest touch of make up on her face she really was exceptionally pretty, and just like last night my cock decided to twitch its approval. Frowning, I shifted my stance slightly; evidently, my 'ultimate control' didn't extend to that part of my anatomy when Stella was around.

'Good evening Stella, come in,' I said, pointedly ignoring the beginnings of an erection. *I am in control*, I reminded myself, not Stella and certainly not my God damn crotch. Settling myself again I stood back to allow her to enter before guiding her to the sofa where I had a bottle of red wine waiting and a notepad ready to jot down the finer points of our agreement.

'I assume you also got the call with the results of your tests? All clear like me?' I asked crisply as I placed down the print out of my results before uncorking the wine. Stella nodded, pulling her own results sheet from her handbag and then briefly passing her gaze over my paperwork. From the corner of my eye I noticed how Stella repeatedly watched me when she thought I wasn't looking. It pleased me immensely to think that she might be as affected by me as I was by her.

'Wine?' Stella confirmed her response with a small silent nod, accepting the glass I offered her. I noticed that unlike my steady fingers Stella's hand was trembling and a sense of masculine pride swept through me at the realisation that it was me causing her to shake.

Once we both had a drink I sat down, probably closer together than Stella might have expected, but I found myself needing to be within her personal space, something rare for me that I think surprised myself as much as it did her.

After taking a sip of wine and finding it very much to my liking I decided to get straight to the point of our evening. 'To summarise the reason for our meeting, you have expressed a wish to enter a sexual relationship as a submissive partner, yes?' Stella nodded jerkily. Her silence was starting to annoy me now, I had enjoyed the sexy tone of her voice last night and wanted to hear more of it, but apparently she was intent on staying quiet for the time being.

Pushing aside her lack of voice, I continued, 'Good,

therefore as an experienced dominant in this meeting I will advise you with what I believe to be suitable limitations or expectations for our time together, but should you wish to add anything please do so.' After a pause, I looked at her again. 'If what I suggest makes you change your mind about our arrangement you must inform me immediately.'

Stella briefly chewed on her bottom lip before nodding her agreement. Bloody silent nods. I was going to order her to speak in a minute just so I could hear the husky, timid whisper that she had used last night when she was nervous. It had been fucking arousing, that whisper. I wanted to hear it again. Needed to.

'To satisfy both our needs it would be best if you stayed here some nights, perhaps just weekends to start with, maybe more if we are both finding the arrangement mutually agreeable. You will have time to work and relax on your own, but staying here would make meeting for our sessions much easier. When you are here, you may treat the apartment as if it were your own, feel free to use the gym, watch the television, whatever pleases you. The only exception is my office; that room is off limits.' Once again, she nodded and I grated my teeth in growing frustration.

'So, shall we start with Friday night to Monday morning?' I suggested before briefly meeting her gaze and seeing Stella nod again. She was obviously nervous, that much was clear, but come on, speak damn it!

'We won't see each other outside of our set times unless there is a good reason or accidental meeting. That will make it easier to maintain our boundaries. I don't want either of us to confuse what we have together as a loving relationship, that's not what it will be. It is simply a mutually agreeable partnership ... but having said that we will be exclusive, neither of us will partake in any form of relationship with anyone else either. This part is very important; I will not share you with any other man. When we meet each weekend I want your pleasure to be heightened by the fact that you have had to wait all week, is that clear and agreeable for you?'

I saw Stella about to nod again and my irritation finally

41

snapped, my voice taking on an autocratic tone as I added my next command. 'If you answer me you need to do so audibly. No more ill-mannered nodding. Understand?'

'Y-yes,' she stuttered. Finally, she speaks! Only one word, but it was a start I suppose. 'Sorry,' she mumbled and I could see in her face that Stella was slightly taken aback by my demanding tone. I almost smiled; if she was expecting something different from me then she was sadly mistaken, I was a dominant through and through, always had been, always would be, and as such I didn't mince my words.

While we were on that subject, I decided to clear up a few other things. 'I'm a naturally serious man, frequently bad-tempered. Don't expect amusing conversation or romance, that's not what I'm about. If I'm in a bad mood you may well be on the receiving end of it, I don't want or expect you to try and cheer me up, just deal with it OK?' My voice sounded a little harsher than I had meant, which was probably due to my frustration at her lack of speech and the growing arousal I was experiencing from talking about our proposed agreement. I watched as Stella's hand took on a light tremble as she sipped her wine and cursed myself for being overly harsh.

'Sure, whatever,' she said giving me a tiny tempting taste of her velvety tone, but although her voice was relatively calm, I could hear an underlying quiver of anxiety that matched her tremble.

Christ, she was such a newbie. Should I play nice and give her an option to get out now? Although the selfish part of me didn't want to, I relented and decided to offer her a chance to leave if she had changed her mind.

'I thrive on complete control over all aspects of my life – my job, my staff, and my submissive. If that's not something that interests you, Stella, you need to leave now.' Almost expecting her to get up and walk out, Stella took me completely by surprise by merely crossing her legs and looking back at me expectantly.

Well, well, I had *not* expected that. Perhaps she was braver than I'd given her credit for. Raising an eyebrow at her casual brush-off of my warning, I continued with the details of our living arrangements. 'I usually cook my evening meals but you may be expected to prepare food on some of the nights you are here, would that be suitable?' I enquired, getting back to the questions that needed discussing and hoping for more than a nod or one word answer.

'Yes, actually I enjoy cooking, I find it relaxes me.' The more casual conversation appeared to be calming Stella and as I enjoyed her husky voice I began to get a glimpse of the woman behind the nerves, a woman who appeared to be quite gutsy and even being inexperienced in submissive relationships would no doubt provide an interesting challenge for me.

'You won't be expected to clean. I have a cleaner, Miranda, she comes twice a week to take care of that. You will however be expected to clear up any mess we make during sex. I like to keep Miranda unaware of the lifestyle I lead.'

'OK.' Stella's voice was quieter now and she blushed at my mention of sex, something I found rather amusing seeing as the entire reason for our meeting was exactly that. The blush itself however was really rather alluring, there was nothing quite like a nice post-orgasmic blush on a pretty face, or a rosy red blushing bottom fresh from a spanking … God, what I wouldn't give to take Stella over my lap now and give her a spanking. *Christ*, my nose flared as I dragged in a desperate breath. I was going to need a cushion over my lap in a minute if I kept thinking like this.

Clearing my throat, I managed to continue but noticed that my voice was huskier than before. 'You will have a room here in my apartment. This is where any physical intimacy will take place – not in my bedroom. Do you have issues sharing a bed for sleeping?' I enquired. The question caused another furious blush to run across Stella's delicate cheeks and fuelled my arousal further.

'Um … n-no,' she stammered before seeming to recover herself. 'Not unless you snore, that is, I'm a pretty light sleeper.' A hint of a smile quirked Stella's lips at her attempt of a joke and the look was so breathtaking that I found myself briefly mirroring the expression before I realised what I was doing and quickly cleared my features. Damn, this woman was affecting me.

'I don't think I do snore,' I answered briskly as way of distraction. Probably a little too briskly – *rudely* – I decided with a grimace. 'As I said earlier, I'm a very private person so I don't like to share my bedroom but I don't see a problem with staying in your room on occasion should either of us want that. It's probably best if it doesn't happen too often though, we don't want the boundaries of our relationship getting blurry.' I'd had more than enough experience of women getting too attached in the past, and was now rather skilled at all the tactics useful in avoiding such incidents; separate bedrooms being one of those tactics.

'OK, sounds sensible,' Stella agreed with a nod. 'What about kissing? Will we kiss?' she asked softly, a fresh blush reddening her cheeks.

In a rare show of my human side I allowed myself a dry chuckle. 'Kissing? You're my submissive, Stella, not a prostitute.' Images of kissing Stella rushed to my mind and I ran a hand through my hair to distract myself, noticing that Stella followed the movement with wide eyes as if perhaps she was holding herself back from touching me. 'I enjoy kissing, so yes, we will kiss, unless you have any objections to it?' I finished. She better not have, I took great pleasure in a good, heated kiss.

Shaking her head, Stella looked embarrassed. 'No. I like it too,' she murmured, flashing a small smile back. I liked that smile of hers, I decided; it was sweet and shy, but sexy as hell.

'So while we're on the topic of physical intimacy we need to discuss our sexual preferences in more detail. My preferences lie in standard sex using some restraining on occasions, but the main factor for me is the need to be in total control, will this be an issue for you?'

'I don't think so. As I said earlier, that's kind of what I'm looking for.' Stella appeared to chew on the inside of her lip as she considered my question and my eyes were immediately drawn to the movement, I didn't like it; if anyone were going to be nibbling on her lips it would be me. I'd let it go for now, but it would be fun to help her break the bad habit once she was

44

officially my submissive.

'You mentioned in the bar yesterday that you like to use punishments, I've not experienced much in that respect, how extreme are we talking?'

'That all depends on how badly you defy me, Stella,' I answered smoothly, well aware that my tone had dropped lower as I considered the very appealing thought of disciplining Stella and her secretly loving every minute of it.

Seeing Stella's eyes widen at my casual response I decided to be generous and elaborate to calm her fears, I didn't want to scare her off before we even got started. 'I will explain all my expectations as we get to know each other, but generally I extend my control with the use of toys and bondage. Remember that in our relationship I will be your dominant, Stella, therefore I will always ensure you are safe in the things we do together. If you ever chose to halt a session for any reason I would always stop immediately.' Pausing I sipped my wine before swilling it round the glass and returning it to the table. 'Now you know that you have control and that your safety is paramount how do you feel about being restrained, tied up?' I questioned intently.

Making some notes on the pad I wondered why Stella hadn't answered and looked up to see a frown of concentration on her face. Apparently, she was thinking things through, which was fine by me. Actually it was rather refreshing to have a submissive that didn't just spout off the answer she thought I would expect. 'I think if we establish trust first then restraining and punishments won't be an issue for me. I know this isn't a standard relationship but I'd like to get to know you a little first before you tie me up,' she finally admitted, but from the way Stella's cheeks flushed I assumed she rather liked the idea of me tying her up. Well, ditto – with images of her pretty little body shackled to the bed writhing below me it was all I could do not to moan out loud.

Seeing Stella shift slightly uncomfortably in her seat I realised something was on her mind and narrowed my eyes; she better not be thinking of changing her mind now because I would be seriously pissed off if she did. 'Is there something you wish to share with me Stella?'

Twisting her hands in her lap Stella shrugged slightly. 'I just thought I should probably warn you that I don't orgasm very easily … it's not a big deal, I mean, I'm used to it now …' She paused, clearly uncomfortable. 'I … I just wanted to let you know.' Her voice was weak by the end of her sentence, embarrassment filling its tone.

What? How the hell could she sound so casual about something as significant as that? Had her previous lovers all been complete imbeciles? 'Never? Or just not often?' I demanded, well aware I sounded astonished that she deemed this fact insignificant.

'During sex I've only ever come in missionary position,' she admitted softly. 'Other positions don't really do it for me, and I've never climaxed from oral or by a man's fingers.'

'I see,' I bit out. Although I didn't really see, I might be demanding in bed but I always ensured the women with me had their pleasure too. How the hell could a man sleep with a beautiful woman like Stella and not make it his mission to give her a climax? Leaning forwards I rested my elbows on my knees and studied her lowered face intently, I couldn't get my head around this new information. *Fuck*, sleeping with her would almost be like taking a virgin and showing her just how good sex can really be. God, the excitement of that thought actually made me feel a little bit light headed.

'What about masturbation? Can you make yourself come using your own hand?' I enquired gruffly.

A fresh blush bloomed on Stella's cheeks that probably matched the heat currently rushing through my own system. 'I can. But then I've had a long time to get used to my body and its peculiarities.'

As she was biting her lip I guessed Stella was desperate for a way to change the subject and I was proved correct when she fired out a random question at me. 'So … will I have a safeword to use? Or a standard body position to assume?'

If that was how she wanted to play it then fine, I'd leave the topic of Stella's climax issues for now, but God I couldn't fucking wait to prove her wrong about her body. There was no way in hell that I wouldn't make her come in every position

46

possible using every single technique I knew. Which was a lot, I thought with a smirk.

Her question came back to me, and I cleared my mind as I tried to focus again, uncomfortably aware that Stella seemed to have a way of distracting me that I couldn't decide if I liked or not.

'Been doing some research on "the scene", have we?' I teased her lightly, but she was still looking a little uncomfortable so I decided not to tease her further. 'In answer to your question, we will have both. The standard safewords are "green" for fine, "yellow" for slight discomfort and "red" for stop. If you say yellow we pause and discuss your concerns, but please be reassured that, regardless of the situation, if you say "red" I will stop immediately.' For this reassurance, I made eye contact with her and felt a surprisingly strong reaction when my eyes met hers. What the hell had that been?

Not feeling entirely comfortable with the sensation that Stella's clear blue gaze had had on me I dropped my eyes again before continuing. 'With regards to your body position, I will know you are ready if you avert your eyes, link your fingers, and allow your hands to hang in front of you or rest in your lap. If I see this position, I know it means you are saying, "I'm ready for instructions".' I paused, deciding to go one step further with Stella, 'I'll coach you to spot my signals too so you will respond to me with no words necessary. For example, if I raise my eyebrow and point to a spot next to me like this,' I demonstrated briefly. 'I will expect you to move to that spot and assume the ready position.

'Many dominants make their subs kneel at their feet. Kneeling is viewed as a very submissive posture.' I remarked while jotting on my pad. 'I believe some of my acquaintances at the club think less of me because I don't demand this,' I pondered out loud before replacing the cap on the pen. Actually there was no 'think' about it, my peers had made their views clear to me, but I didn't give a toss what they thought – I had reasons for my choices and to have my submissive standing was one of them.

After a brief pause where I watched Stella chew on her lip

again – I was definitely going to make breaking that habit one of my first priorities – she then licked her lips and spoke. 'I can kneel if you would like it?' she offered, a statement that I found ridiculously pleasing, not that I wanted her to kneel, but just because she was willing to offer it to me.

A shudder went through me as images flashed in my mind of my father looming over my helpless brother as he knelt on the floor. Swallowing the bile that suddenly rose in my throat I shook my head. 'No, the position we have discussed is fine,' I said sharply. 'Kneeling makes the sub smaller, more akin to a child or an animal, both of which are easy to command or overpower. I gain satisfaction from the knowledge that I can leave my subs standing up and still have complete control over them.' My brother Nicholas often told me that he thought I was similar to my father, but in this one respect, I was most definitely *not* like my father.

As I spoke I watched in fascination as Stella experimented with the position by linking her hands in her lap. As she averted her eyes the stray wisps of her tied up hair hung around her face and the soft curve of her shoulder became much more obvious. Suddenly my chest felt full and tight as I tried, and failed, to draw in a full breath. *Fuck me,* she was glorious.

Stella looked perfect, and the sight made my arousal soar through the roof, so much so that I had to fight back the urge to push her back on the sofa and take her there and then.

Clearing my throat gruffly and shifting my position to alleviate the tightness in my trousers, I tried once again to distract my bloody wandering thoughts. 'You may have noticed that I don't like extended eye contact,' I stated coolly, may as well get this out in the open now, I saw Stella nod, a small frown settling on her brows indicating to me that she obviously had noticed. 'This is nothing personal against you, it stems from issues in my past that I won't bore you with, but it's important that you avoid prolonged eye contact with me.' After growing up with my father, I rarely made eye contact with anyone now, except Nicholas.

'I'll do my best; you might need to remind me though because eye contact is a big thing for me. You can tell a lot about a person from their eyes, I use it in business a lot to judge clients' honesty.'

I drew in a breath through my nose. I had no idea what she meant. How could you read someone through their eyes? Why had I never been allowed to learn this as a child? It was like a huge life skill had been withheld from me by my father, but if I were honest the idea of trying to learn it now scared the hell out of me, unnerved me beyond anything else I'd ever experienced.

Well, that change in conversation had certainly cooled my lust and now I found myself shifting uncomfortably on the sofa trying to loosen off the tension that had suddenly formed in my shoulders.

'I'm sure I can think of a way or two to remind you if you forget,' I murmured ominously to steer the subject away from myself. *Ha!* It obviously worked because I saw Stella shiver at my threat. A dark smile broke on my lips at her obvious fear; what an excellent response from a new submissive.

'Ah, the discipline.' Stella guessed in a wary tone with a cautious nod. Visibly loosening her shoulders, I watched as she corrected her position and sat a little straighter in her chair. She really did have rather pleasing posture. My eyes narrowed and I moistened my lips as I watched her small adjustments. With posture like that Stella's muscle structure was bound to be strong and flexible; good, even better for what I had in mind for her. A smirk curled my lip. Christ, I loved a woman who held herself well; it was just so sexy to see them so confident, but still willing to submit to me.

'So I'm curious ...' Stella began, she was anxiously twisting a silver ring on her thumb and looking hesitant enough to make me wonder what the hell she was going to say next. 'What type of stuff are we talking about? Will it involve pain, because I read about sadists on the Internet and it was pretty freaky stuff ...' Ah, good, so she was curious about exactly how I would punish her. It was something that was on my mind too; with Stella the options just seemed limitless at the moment and once again I found myself having to shift my position to ease the pressure on my goddamn groin. Explaining things like this was all new to me; I was used to trained subs who rarely asked more than one or two questions before signing our agreement. It was actually quite refreshing to see Stella's obvious intelligence and curiosity shining through, but she also looked quite uncomfortable at the moment.

'Relax Stella,' I said quickly, 'I use spankings as a punishment on occasion, but this is nothing like the sadists you saw on the internet. I'm not a sadist.' I assured her firmly, 'Inflicting severe pain holds no interest for me, like I said I get my kicks from control in the bedroom.' I liked a little spanking and often used a paddle or flogger to redden up a nice bottom, but more as a way of heightening pleasure than inflicting any excessive pain. Probably just as well if Stella's reaction was anything to go by.

'Right.' Stella still looked slightly troubled, but also relieved by my statement. I noticed she still took a rather large gulp of her wine none the less. 'So for you, you like control ... but what would be your daily expectations, and what would be a really dominant thing for you to do?' Stella hiccupped a dry laugh; a strange noise which made my eyebrows rise. 'Sorry, that question doesn't even make sense to me ...' she mumbled around a shy smile and I rather enjoyed watching as her cheeks flushed yet again.

'Your articulation was not the most eloquent, Stella,' I agreed with a disapproving frown, 'but I know what you were getting at – you want to know what I will expect of you, what I will do with you.' Lust lowered the tone on my last six words. Oh God ... the *things* I wanted to do with Stella.

I let out a harsh breath and cleared my mind. 'While I appreciate that people find me an intimidating presence to be around I think the things that appeal to me are in fact relatively simple; having you respond to my requests promptly, comply with them, and give yourself over to my control will be my daily expectations.' Taking a sip of my wine I briefly wondered about telling her why control was so important to me, especially with the recent flashbacks I'd been having, but I promptly decided against it with a grimace – she didn't need to hear the pitiful story spoken out loud. 'You probably won't like the way this sounds, but I almost want to feel like I own you, like you are mine to do whatever I want with. Within the bounds of our consensual agreement, of course,' I added.

I had suspected that Stella's nerves had been rising over the last few minutes, but this time her large swallow was actually audible to me. Ah well, her discomfort couldn't be helped, I decided with a sip of wine, it was best she knew what I expected from the start. 'While you are here you are free to do as you wish unless I request you to come to me. As such, you won't need permission for day to day things, but for the sake of formality I would ask that you refer to me as 'Sir' whenever we are together. Is that something you could do?'

After a brief pause where she chewed on her damn lip again, she then looked up at me. 'Is all this stuff up for discussion? Like a compromise?' Stella asked, completely throwing me. What the fuck? I'd never, ever, *ever* had a submissive trying to bargain with me. Before refusing her request I forced myself to count down from five in my head as I considered her words. It had been obvious from the start that things with Stella were going to be different, so perhaps if it kept her happy and made her more pliable I could make a concession, although that would depend on exactly what she proposed.

'Perhaps. State your terms,' I replied coolly, not entirely comfortable with this new dynamic to our relationship, I was supposed to be the one in charge, the dominant, not some bartering salesman.

'Well ... I ...' she paused, apparently wondering how to proceed, which left me even more intrigued. 'I don't mind calling you Sir, that's fine, it's just that this is all new to me and I think I might forget to do it sometimes and I don't want to be continually punished for it ... would it be possible for me just to use it when we were ... you know ...' she shifted awkwardly on the sofa, indicating her growing discomfort, '... in the bedroom?' She finally finished in a whisper.

Considering her statement, I narrowed my eyes as I thought it through. Technically the title of Sir wasn't what turned me on, it was the submission and control aspect that did it for me. Over the years, the title had just kind of come along with it, but still, could I really compromise with her on this? It was a very alien consideration for me.

'You'd still be in control of me at all other times, I just think that maybe that way I wouldn't let you down as much.' She added softly, linking her fingers in her lap as if to prove her point. *I'd still be in control*, fuck, her words hit on exactly the reason for my hesitation, it was like she somehow knew me far more intimately then she possibly could. Her second little sentence about not letting me down was pretty well worded too; the fact that she seemed keen to please me was very satisfying indeed.

'But you'll use the title when we are together sexually?' I confirmed stiffly.

Stella nodded. 'Yes ... *Sir,* whenever we are in the bedroom,' she said, apparently testing out the title. God it sounded good coming from her mouth.

'Fine, we can try that to start with,' I acquiesced and jotted it down on the pad. Who said I couldn't be reasonable? 'I should warn you though that our liaisons may not only occur in the bedroom, Stella, but regardless of where I chose to take you I expect you to call me Sir if we are having sex.'

'OK,' she agreed, a crimson flush spreading on her cheeks that I suspected came from lust, not embarrassment this time. I knew exactly how she felt, blood was rushing to my groin so fast right now that it was all I could do not to groan and rub my poor ignored hard-on to give it some relief.

Ever the professional, I had been making notes of our agreed terms as we spoke, but continued to write as I explained more about what my expectations for our relationship would be. 'Sometimes our meetings will just be regular sex, sometimes bondage or occasional punishments if I see fit. We will eat meals together and do various other things during the periods that you stay here but I want to reiterate the fact that you shouldn't expect long conversations or romance. It won't happen. If you want that, you need to seek out a dom with the same intentions.'

Once again, I paused to give Stella a chance to express the wish to leave, but she simply sat silently and I thanked my lucky stars before continuing. 'I will expect you to maintain immaculate hygiene levels at all times, hands washed before every meal, no hair under your arms or on your legs. I would prefer your groin hairless, but if you are uncomfortable with that then trimmed short will be fine.'

Dotting the final full stop, I held up the notepad with our agreed terms and indicated to it with a jerk of my chin. 'Obviously this isn't legally binding, it's more of an understanding that we can refer to at any point. If either of us wishes to end our agreement we can simply say so and tear up the contract, end of,' I stated firmly. 'If you are happy with what we have discussed then we can start next Friday, I'll get it typed up before then so you can sign it and have a copy to keep.' It was Sunday today so that would give me plenty of time to type up the contract and set up a room for Stella within the apartment.

'OK.' Pausing, Stella flexed the little finger on her right hand so it brushed against my thigh causing a tingle of anticipation to rush up my leg and settle in my already tortured groin. What the hell was this woman trying to do to me? I sucked in a sharp breath and then tilted my head to look across at her. She was innocently averting her eyes as I'd asked, but I couldn't help but wonder if she also felt the sizzling electricity between us. Perhaps she'd even brushed my leg on purpose?

A bubble of excitement settled in my stomach. I couldn't remember the last time I'd found a submissive that not only had similar bedroom tastes to me, but with whom I had also shared a true physical connection with. In fact, had it ever happened? With my looks, I'd always managed to find attractive submissives, physically speaking. But had any of my previous partners caused my body to react like this? After taking a second to think back through the women who had, for various lengths of time, shared my life, I shook my head, no, I didn't think so. I frowned, that probably wasn't a good thing was it? Perhaps I should do the sensible thing and end this before it got out of hand.

Nah, fuck that. I wanted Stella and I planned on having her, regardless of the consequences. Thanks to David at Club Twist this chance meeting with Stella could lead to a very satisfying relationship for both of us. The prospect of the things we could do together made my heart accelerate tenfold under my skin which was crazy seeing as we knew so little about each other, but already there was a spark firing between us, making it almost impossible to think about anything other than pushing my throbbing dick inside her, and what was even better was that I'd almost place money on the fact that Stella was feeling the chemistry too.

Breaking my thoughts Stella shifted slightly in her seat, her eyes briefly flicking to mine before lowering again. 'It seems a very long time until next Friday, Sir,' Stella murmured softly, the word 'Sir' practically purring from her tongue and sending an instant rush of blood to my painfully hard groin.

Holy fuck, I'd been right, Stella wanted me just as much as I wanted her, right before my eyes she'd flipped into proper submissive mode and I seriously thought it might be the sexiest thing I'd ever seen. The thought did nothing whatsoever to calm my thundering erection, but always the professional I tried my best to be practical about the situation.

Indicating to the agreement on the coffee table, I pursed my lips. 'We need to do a bit of training, first, build up our trust, Stella. Plus this isn't typed up and signed yet,' I muttered, for once hating myself and my stupidly obsessive ways.

Hell, if I didn't relieve the tension in my groin soon I was going to burst through my trousers. There was no doubt about it; I was going to need a seriously cold shower when Stella had gone. Normally if I was this horny I'd get a willing woman to pop over and ease my frustration, but as I was now strictly monogamous in my relationships that wasn't an option any more. Perhaps I'd have to resort to my own right hand for some relief later tonight.

Taking me completely by surprise Stella leant forwards, plucked the pen from my hand, and neatly signed her name under the list of agreed points before sitting back with her hands in her lap, fingers twined just as I had told her to do so when she was ready for instructions. *Holy shit*, I was so light-headed from the blood pounding in my cock that I started to worry that I might have a brain malfunction at any minute.

Clenching my teeth I briefly fought the dilemma in my head; I never started a sexual relationship with a submissive until everything was officially arranged, *never*. Although Stella had just signed the hand-written version of the agreement, so technically it *was* official. Plus she'd passed the STI tests, so really there was no reason not to indulge in a little sample tonight, was there? I could always start with the training next week …

Glancing at Stella's quietly expectant pose again, I allowed myself a small smile. This woman was going to keep me on my toes, that much was already abundantly clear. She was sexually submissive, yes, but being an independent businesswoman, she no doubt had enough backbone to challenge even me, a thought that thrilled me immensely. Shaking my head in mild amusement I gave in to the internal debate in my head and shifted myself to face her on the sofa.

'I wasn't expecting all this to happen tonight Stella, so the room you'll use isn't ready,' I informed her, my voice low and gritty from the strain of holding myself back. 'However, I think perhaps before I drop you home we could seal our agreement here on the sofa, test for compatibility, so to speak.'

I heard a soft gasp escape from Stella that was so fucking sexy it very nearly sent me over the edge right there and then, but like an ultimate submissive, she didn't react with any other outward response, merely sat waiting for my instructions.

Where to start? There was so much I wanted to do with Stella. A myriad of possibilities was flooding through my mind, making me giddy like a kid in a sweet shop.

If there was ever a time when I needed my mantra it was now. *I am in control.* I repeated it several times in my head gathering my composure and then smoothly rose from the sofa. My raging hard on must be blatantly obvious to Stella, but I didn't care, she'd be getting up close and personal with it soon enough.

'Stand up.' I heard the way my tone had instinctively dropped as I switched on my truly dominant mode and wondered if Stella would pick up on it too. Probably, I decided, as I watched her push herself upright in front of me. She stood with a straight, confident back but with her eyes wide and turned down and hands loosely twined in front of her.

Fucking perfection. 'Let your hair down,' I ordered softly. Almost immediately, Stella reached up and began to un-clip the multitude of pins that she must have painstakingly slipped into her hair before her meeting with me. It looked good up, but I couldn't wait to feel how soft it would be when I wrapped my hands in it.

Once the clips were removed, I watched as Stella ran her hands through her long, blonde hair to loosen its soft waves before linking her hands in front of herself again.

My throat was constricted with lust now, feeling like it was thick with cotton wool, but I forced myself on. 'Undress. Start with your top.' Once again, Stella followed my instructions without hesitation, a very good start. She gripped the hem of her camisole and ran her fingers around it, tempting me by displaying several little glimpses of her flat stomach before finally pulling it over her head gracefully. After tossing it aside she flattened out her hair and linked her fingers as she stilled, awaiting my next command.

This was fucking torture, every fibre in my body was screaming at me to throw her on the floor and take her like the animal that I was, but I persevered, delaying my gratification would only make the prize at the end even more delectable. 'My shirt next,' I instructed huskily. I normally liked to undress myself, but the temptation Stella was offering tonight was just too great. Lifting her fingers Stella began to deftly undo my shirt buttons and I noticed in admiration that even with the adrenaline of our first encounter her fingers weren't shaking.

Stella might be a successful businesswoman, but she was proving that she was also a seemingly perfect, shy submissive. Just by being here in my apartment tonight, she had proved that underneath her well-presented façade she clearly had an exciting experimental streak that I couldn't wait to help her explore.

'Slowly,' I reminded her, as Stella suddenly started to tug a little impatiently on the fourth button of my shirt. A smile curled my lips – maybe she wasn't quite as cool and collected as she was making out.

Once my shirt was unbuttoned Stella tugged it out from my trousers and pushed it open, one of her hands accidentally brushed across my chest as she did so, causing both of us to gasp as electricity zinged between us from the first occurrence of skin on skin contact. Jesus, that had been incredible. Automatically Stella looked up at me in surprise. Caught off guard, I met her gaze and saw that her eyes were wide and expectant and dilated with desire, as mine must surely be too. Apparently remembering herself Stella blinked as she dropped her gaze to my chest where she pressed one hand flat on my stomach and trailed her fingers experimentally through the soft hair there.

Fucking hell, her touch felt so amazing. I wasn't going to last a minute if that hand dropped any lower.

Inhaling sharply I absorbed the delicious feeling of her touch for a few more seconds before reaching down and removing Stella's hand. Thanks to my thriving business it had been six months since I'd been with a woman and I damn well wasn't going to lose control like a like a randy teenager.

'It would appear we have rather good chemistry, Stella. Perhaps our agreement will be even more enjoyable than we first thought,' I murmured before giving her the next prompt. 'Take off your skirt.'

Obliging me immediately Stella peeled herself out of her ridiculously tight skirt and then stood in front of me wearing nothing but some very skimpy black lace underwear. It was marginally see through and such a turn on I had to clench my fists to stop myself reaching out for her. 'Step back, I want to see you,' I encouraged, before I allowed my eyes to roam across all the curves and planes of Stella's smoking hot body.

God she had a seriously great figure: long legs, curvy waist, pert full breasts, and creamy skin that I immediately wanted to taste. Not just taste … I wanted to nip and lick and mark her as mine. How the hell I'd got so lucky I still had no idea. Beauty, intellect, chemistry, and now a body to die for. I really, *really* needed to phone David Halton in the morning and thank him. Hell, maybe I'd send a casket of decent whisky over too.

Wasting no more time I removed my trousers and stepped towards her wearing just my black boxer shorts, which by now were seriously straining to contain my jutting erection. Breathing more shallowly than I could ever remember I slipped my hands into the hair by her temples then raised my arms and allowed it to flow through my fingers like silk. Jesus, that felt so good I just had to do it again, before the urge to kiss her overwhelmed me and I suddenly tangled my right hand through a section of hair and dragged her head forwards until her mouth collided with mine.

I kissed Stella with all the pent-up exasperation I had been feeling ever since I'd met her yesterday and so my kiss was far from soft, but hell if it wasn't exactly what I needed at that particular moment. My grip on her hair was no doubt painful, but I had never been a gentle lover so Stella may as well get used to it from the outset. A soft moan of approval escaped between her lips and any concerns I may have had about her disliking my rough treatment faded away. *She was just perfect.* Stella stumbled forwards closer into my embrace and melded her body against mine, gasping in obvious pleasure as our bodies collided from my sudden onslaught.

Using Stella's gasp I gained entry to her hot tempting mouth, my tongue moving against hers for the first time as they twisted and tangled furiously. Aware of the fact that I might well bruise her lips if I didn't calm down I forced myself to soften the kiss, but maintained the tight grip on her hair to ensure she couldn't pull away, not that she seemed to want to; quite the opposite, in fact, if her heated response was anything to go by.

Finally ripping my mouth from hers I found Stella gazing up at me. Panting, she raised a hand and ran a trembling finger across her swollen lips making me lick my own in response, but her eyes lingered on mine for far longer than I was comfortable with so I quickly tugged on her hair tipping her head backwards and forcing her gaze away from me.

'Sorry, Sir.' She mumbled, apparently realising her mistake with the eye contact. A very pleasing response, so I forgave her immediately. Her breath was just as ragged as mine, and with her head tilted back this way I could actually see Stella's pulse fluttering in the thin skin on her neck like a hummingbird's frantic wings. Christ, she was just as turned on as me. This whole situation really was fucking unbelievable.

Her neck was just too tempting so lowering my head I grazed my teeth along her pulse point before kissing her soft skin, sucking on her neck, gently biting on her earlobe, and finally running my tongue across her pulse tasting her skin as I'd wanted to. She tasted lightly floral with just a touch of salt and I couldn't help but drag her even closer to my mouth so I could get some more. A shudder ran through her entire body and Stella let out a soft whimper as her body seemed to respond instinctively to my contact near her ear.

'Do you like that, Stella? To be kissed just here?' I asked heatedly, keen to learn her body and repeating my treatment of her earlobe and finishing by running my tongue across the sensitive skin of her neck again.

'Ahh, yes.' Stella's response was breathy against my hair, but I immediately noticed the absence of 'Sir'. Seeing as she had made me agree to her only using the title during sex there was no way I was going to let her slip go unnoticed so I gave her hair another firm tug which had Stella yelping before quickly correcting herself. 'Yes, Sir.' *Good*, she was a quick learner, I observed with pleasure.

Without giving Stella any warning, I stepped back completely, removing all contact between us and then clenched my fists. 'Take off your underwear before I rip it off,' I instructed in nothing short of a growl, and my words weren't far from the truth – I wanted to fuck her so badly now that it was taking every ounce of my self-control not to throw her on the floor and simply take her.

My tongue was practically hanging out of my mouth like a thirsty dog as I watched Stella slowly tuck her thumbs into the elastic of her lacy knickers and ease them down her thighs before letting them drop to the floor. Forgetting to watch the delicate way she managed to step out of them I instead found myself completely fixated on the apex of her thighs. I couldn't believe it, she was practically hairless, just a thin strip of hair marked her entrance, exactly how I liked it. Could she be any more perfect for me, I wondered as I unashamedly gazed at her near nakedness?

Mind you, I'd better wait and see how Stella reacted to my more extreme bedroom behaviour before I judged how perfect a match we were; she might run screaming once I'd chained her up a few times, I realised, clenching my teeth at the delicious image of Stella bound and restrained below me.

Reaching behind herself Stella undid her bra next, the movement caused her breasts to jut forward and I dug my nails painfully into my palms with the effort not to drag the damn thing from her body. Finally, she slid the straps down her arms and the bra fell to the floor leaving Stella stood naked in front of me, panting breathlessly.

She wasn't the only one panting. She was so damn sexy that I was struggling to blink. I was struggling to breathe ... fuck, I was struggling to function, full stop. I needed to chill out or I'd blow my load right here and now. Drawing in a breath, I counted down from five to zero in my head. I usually only used my countdowns when I was pissed off and close to punching something, or someone, but tonight it was for an altogether different reason – my sanity, and Stella's safety, God knows how rough I'd be if I leapt on her now and took her without calming down first.

'Christ, Stella, you have a fabulous body,' I murmured huskily, I always made a point of complimenting my submissives, I'd found over the years that they tended to be more pliant if they felt good about themselves, but tonight with Stella my words were nothing but the truth. Her body was curvy but firm, with those long legs that would be perfect for wrapping around my waist in the throes of passion and a tempting chest that I could no longer resist.

'Thank you, Sir,' she murmured softly, the velvet of her tone spurring me on.

Swiftly removing my boxer shorts, I closed the gap between us and took Stella completely by surprise by scooping her into my arms and depositing her roughly back on the sofa behind us. Catching both of her wrists in one of my hands was easy, they were so tiny compared to my palms, and I wasted no time pinning them above her head and lowering my mouth to her left breast that had been tempting me for so long.

Twirling my tongue around the rosy nipple, I felt it harden instantly and Stella let out a soft mewling sound as her back arched off the sofa up towards me. What a pleasing response, I thought with a smirk, so I rewarded her keenness with a hard suckle that made her squirm below me before I changed my attentions to Stella's other full breast, using my teeth to roughly tug the nipple to its full length.

While my mouth was busy with her delightful breasts my free hand explored the softness of her stomach and thighs before slipping lower to run along the line of hair leading to her pussy. By this point, Stella was writhing below me making frustrated sounds of desperation and so I raised my head, keeping my gaze on her beautiful full lips as I spoke. 'Would you like me to take you straight away, Stella, or shall I play for longer?'

'Now, Sir,' she breathed heavily, her body still squirming below me. '*Please.*' Apparently, the little strip tease had also got Stella just as worked up as I felt.

'I rather like the sound of you begging me, Stella,' I murmured, lowering my lips to hers as my free hand moved lower to tease the already soaked folds between her legs, Christ, she was so wet for me. 'Say it again, tell me what you want,' I encouraged her gruffly, finally releasing her hands so they could roam across my back.

'You. Please, I want you, Sir.'

'Good. We'll stick to missionary for tonight; I want you to climax too.' Tackling the issue of her inability to climax in other positions would have to wait for another evening because even if I had wanted to draw out the process longer, I couldn't have done it for the world. My self-control was already at breaking point so as Stella pleaded with me again to take her, I did, moving myself above her and sliding into her wet darkness in one smooth stroke. I paused briefly to savour the sensation of her warm tightness before starting up a fierce rhythm that had Stella digging her nails into my back and spurring me on with her soft moans as our hips clashed together furiously.

Wanting to lose myself in the sensation and thrust with abandon I only just managed to hold myself back. I could be a fierce lover at times, aggressive and powerful, but even in my lust-fuelled state I was vaguely aware that I didn't want to hurt Stella and scare her off.

Perhaps she read my mind, or maybe Stella and I were just more perfectly suited than I could ever have dared hope, because the next words out of her mouth were just astounding. 'Harder, Sir … Please … harder …'

I was already thrusting into her almost savagely, but apparently my new little sub wanted more, just like I did. Well hell, I thought, bring it on. Dropping my left leg onto the floor I planted my foot firmly and using the new leverage practically pile drove myself into her, pistoning my hips like a madman with such force that it shunted Stella up the sofa with each thrust.

With this new deeper position, it wasn't long until I felt Stella tightening below me. 'Wait … don't climax until I say …' I panted harshly, knowing I was close and wanting our first time to be as explosive as possible. Three more deep thrusts were all it took. 'Now!' I demanded, and as my hot climax began to spurt into her unbelievably receptive body, I felt Stella's inner muscles clenching around my shaft so fucking hard I thought I might burst as she too found her release, gasping and moaning feverishly below me.

Hell, if the explosiveness of this first time was anything to go by this woman was going to be the death of me.

SEVEN – STELLA

The morning, after my escapade with Nathan – or should that be sex-capade? – I woke up later than usual, something I fully blamed on Nathan and the exhausting workout he had given me on the sofa. Luckily, I managed to escape to work without seeing Kenny, the king of gossip, who I knew would have tried to grill me for details and make me even later than I already was. Once at work I ensconced myself in my office and found that the morning flew by, mostly because I did no work whatsoever and instead focused on replaying every minute of my naughty night with Nathan.

My desk phone rang just after half past eleven, interrupting me from replaying my delicious orgasm for the hundredth time, and I picked it up with a frown muttering my usual greeting feeling rather annoyed at the interruption.

'Stella, there's a guy here in reception demanding to see you.' I recognised the voice as Zara, a new employee on reception that I was starting to get friendly with. Briefly my brain leapt to the farfetched conclusion that it might be Nathan coming to see me, desperate for a replay of last night and unable to wait until Friday, but then Zara continued with a giggled whisper. 'I've never seen dress sense quite like this ... he's wearing pink trousers, a red shirt, and a blue tie ... it kind of suits him though ...' she pondered, her voice dropping off. I rolled my eyes, it wasn't Nathan then, he wouldn't be seen dead in that get up, no, the only person I knew who dressed that appallingly and managed to carry it off with style was Kenny.

As soon as the lift doors opened, I saw Kenny leaning against the reception counter doing his best impression of flirting with Zara. For an out and out gay guy he certainly knew how to charm the ladies. Although with striking good looks like his I suspected it was never too difficult for him with either sex, because Kenny was lucky enough to have a Johnny Depp look about him; angular features, vivid green eyes, a neatly trimmed goatee, and chin-length shiny black hair, all in all the perfect package ... except for his preference for men, of course, which was a bit of an obstacle if you were a hot blooded female hoping to strike it lucky with him. Sure enough as I got closer I could see Zara blushing and giggling with him as they spoke and I shook my head, he was such a tease.

'Ah, here she is!' Kenny turned back to Zara and leant towards her conspiratorially as if they were best buddies. 'Can you believe Stella went on a hot date last night and didn't tell me the details before she left for work this morning?' he confided with mock disapproval in his tone. 'So I've come to take you for lunch,' he announced, turning to me and holding out an arm. He would probably make a scene if I declined, so I rolled my eyes and took his arm, but not before noting the look of interest that Zara was giving me. Marvellous, she'd probably ask me about my 'date' later and I'd have to lie to her. What a great way to start a friendship.

As soon as we were through the revolving doors and out onto the busy street I turned to him and lightly smacked him on the arm. 'Kenny! I don't want the people I work with to know I'm dating anyone.' Not that it was exactly dating. I grimaced as I considered exactly what it was I had started with Nathan ... Sex, I suppose, just with a written contract and a few rules thrown in the mix.

Kenny was the only person I had told about my arrangement with Nathan, I'd explained the bizarre link between Nathan's company and where I worked to Kenny and had planned on keeping the whole thing on the down low, but that might be a bit trickier now thanks to Kenny's big mouth.

'Whatever,' he scoffed with a dismissive wave of his hand. 'If you're that bothered just tell anyone who asks that you went out on a date with a guy but have decided not to see him again.' He led me across the road towards the park. 'I thought we'd go to that new deli on George Street,' he added. 'Nina's, is it?' He named a café that was just round the corner from my work and famed for its amazing sandwiches and salads.

Once we were seated and had ordered; tomato and mozzarella salad for me, a spinach and aubergine smoothie for Kenny – *ugh* – he leant forward with a familiar twinkle in his eye. 'Come on then, my girl, spill the beans, you dashed out of the house awfully quick this morning which I took to mean "I got laid last night when I promised I wouldn't".' He smirked at me knowingly and my traitorous cheeks immediately flushed bright red.

'Ah-ha! I knew it, you little tartlet,' he joked playfully as he flicked his napkin onto his lap. 'Come on then, let's have the juicy gossip!' Just because Kenny was always happy to share the details of his conquests with me – sometimes with *way* too many details – didn't mean I wanted to do the same, especially not while sat in a packed café, but as he flashed me his puppy dog eyes I sighed and eventually gave in. It would be nice to have a guy's perspective on things, besides, I could talk freely with Kenny seeing as he was the one to persuade me into all this craziness in the first place.

'Well … we started off discussing the terms of our agreement, limits, expectations, that sort of thing,' I said, pausing as the waitress delivered our food, my salad and Kenny's slop, my lip curled. God that smoothie looked positively gag-worthy. I truly would never understand these fad diets he went on.

'I was so nervous that at first I kept nearly giggling at how business-like he was being,' I told Kenny in a whisper. 'Like I was a deal he was trying to broker, except instead of buildings or bonds, I was the object being acquired.'

'I suppose, given who you're dealing with, that's kind of the case,' Kenny said, taking a sip of his hideous-looking drink and attempting to hide his disgusted face. I on the other hand couldn't hide my smirk.

'So was he just as gorgeous as you remembered?' Kenny asked, pushing aside his drink and leaning over to pinch a piece of my mozzarella. Cheeky bugger, he always did this when he was dieting, I really didn't know why he bothered with the pretence.

'Yep. More so,' I murmured, probably slightly dreamily, but then I felt myself getting irritable as Kenny got his mobile out and started fiddling with it. Must be a text message. Charming, he'd dragged me out here supposedly keen to hear my gossip but now his frigging phone was more important.

'Oh. My. God.' Kenny separated each word with a significant pause and his awed tone made me look up from my salad. His eyes flicked to mine and narrowed. 'Is this him? Because if it is I'm going to be severely pissed off with you.'

I was totally confused now, what the hell was Kenny on about? Snatching his phone I looked at the picture on the screen and drew in a quick breath before my cheeks flushed with pleasure.

The screen to Kenny's phone was filled with an image of Nathan in all his glory. Using my finger to scroll around the page I realised that when Kenny had been fiddling with his phone he'd actually been doing a quick Google search for Nathan. The page displayed was the corporate staff listing for Nathaniel Jackson Architecture, featuring every member of staff, reviewing their qualifications and providing one photograph. Nathan's was simply glorious. Dressed in a grey three-piece suit with a white shirt and black tie, Nathan was staring intently at the camera with a slight frown on his face and looked every bit the corporate executive, and every bit the dominant lover I'd experienced last night. A shiver of pleasure ran through me as I gripped Kenny's phone tighter in my suddenly clammy hand.

'That's him,' I murmured, trying not to dribble on the phone as I placed two fingers on the screen and opened them up to zoom in on Nathan's breathtaking features. Suddenly Kenny's earlier comment came back to me and I frowned. 'Hang on, why are you going to be pissed off with me?' Not that I really believed he'd be pissed off with me – Kenny's approach to life was so laid back he was pretty much horizontal, and as such rarely held grudges or moods for long.

'Because I've never bedded a man that god-like. It's not

fair,' Kenny grumbled on a pout before snatching his phone back and examining the picture of Nathan again. In the blink of an eye, Kenny's strop was gone as his eyes lit up as he looked to me expectantly. 'Please tell me that he was just as god-like in bed?'

'He was,' I confirmed a touch smugly with a nod. 'Exceedingly god-like in the sex department.' Then, on a giggle, I remembered back to last night and decided to tease Kenny with one more morsel before I had to get back to work. 'Except we didn't actually make it as far as the bed, but I can definitely confirm that as far as rampant sofa shags go he's the best I've ever had.' What was it about Kenny that brought out my inner slut! 'Thanks for lunch, Ken, but I gotta get back, see you tonight,' I mumbled as I popped my last bit of mozzarella into my mouth and left Kenny with his jaw hanging open in shock, his barely touched smoothie in his hand.

EIGHT – NATHAN

All through primary and secondary school, I was bullied and taunted because of my introverted ways and avoidance of eye contact. When my brother Nicholas was old enough to join me at school, he had fared no better. In fact, the teasing had got so bad that it wasn't often that I even bothered to interact with other pupils. Judgemental tossers, the lot of them.

By the time I had reached college at the age of 17, I still had no real friends and had never even dared look at a girl. From listening in to the conversations in the lunch hall, I knew some of the guys in my class had girlfriends who they kissed and touched, but I had found it impossible to imagine how such a relationship could develop between two people. My role models were my parents and although they did sometimes kiss each other or hold hands, I also knew that my father's beatings extended beyond myself and my brother to my mother too. Was that how it was supposed to be between a man and woman?

Completely coincidentally, this question was inadvertently answered for me later the very next month on a drizzly Sunday. Sunday nights were 'early to bed nights' in the Jackson household, with both me and Nicholas in our rooms by 9 p.m. As well as being early to bed night, Sunday was special to myself and Nicholas because it was also the only night in the week when we wouldn't receive a beating; in fact our father wouldn't come to our rooms at all. I had thought this might be because it was God's day, but whatever the reason I was always thankful for the extra smiles I got from my little brother on a Sunday.

Knowing I shouldn't have had an extra glass of lemonade with dinner, I sat on the edge of my bed and wondered if I could hold my pee until the morning. It had only just gone half past nine, my mother had bid me goodnight half an hour ago, but I knew if my father caught me out of bed so soon after curfew that I would be in for a punishment regardless of what day of the week it was.

Squirming on my bed for another few seconds, I decided that at age 17 wetting my bed really wasn't an option, so I abruptly stood up and crept to the door. Opening it as quietly as I could I thanked God that the temperamentally squeaky handle had miraculously remained silent tonight as I pulled it open.

Tiptoeing along the corridor, I paused when I heard pained gasps whisper in the air. Spinning towards Nicholas' bedroom, I hurried to check that my father wasn't breaking his Sunday rule, but as I peeked in the darkened room all I could hear was Nicholas snoring lightly.

Frowning, I crept back towards my parents' bedroom. The door was ajar but it was forbidden for me to enter so I went to make my way past to get to the toilet when another more fevered moan of pain reached my ears. After hesitating for just a second or so on the threshold I peered in the crack of the door.

My eyes widened at the sight before me. My mother was completely naked on the bed facing away from me crouched on her hands and knees. Her thighs, buttocks, and the majority of her back were glowing an angry red colour, marked with a criss-cross of feint welt like marks.

Marks like mine.

For a second or two I was unable to comprehend what I was seeing, I was torn between the perversity of looking at my mother naked and the overwhelming desire to assess the criss-cross of marks on her skin that were so similar to the ones that often coloured my own body after my father's beatings. Just then, my father stepped into view, fully dressed and holding something in his hand that seemed to have 10 or 12 thin leather straps attached to it. I had no idea what it was, but it certainly wasn't the belt that he used on my brother and I. He raised his hand, and I knew he was about to bring the implement down on my mother's buttocks.

I was considering going in to help my mother, but I was too

70

afraid of what the consequences might be if I intervened. Would he turn that awful whip thing on me too?

Not wanting to witness the unsavoury sight of my parents together, I had stumbled on to the bathroom in shock. As I staggered away, I was surprised to hear my mother moan again, but even to my sexually inexperienced ears it was quite obviously a moan of pleasure. Was that normal? Usual behaviour between a husband and wife? Perhaps it was. After all, my father always told me that the beatings I received were no different to the ones my friends would be getting at home too. Not that, as 'Freakoid Jackson', I had any friends to ask of course.

After so long of being controlled by my father I was becoming keen on the idea of breaking free and extending my own control somehow. Perhaps it was teenage hormones kicking in, but lately I had been thinking about getting a girlfriend of my own.

Wanting to know that the beating and sex between my parents hadn't just been a one-off I had crouched outside my parents' bedroom door on several Sunday evenings to see if they always engaged in the same activity. Thankfully the sight of my parents fucking never aroused me, but I watched because I thought that perhaps this was important for my development as a man, after all I was nearly 18 now, and like any red-blooded boy my age, I was intrigued by the idea of sex.

My findings were conclusive; although the positions they took were often different, the outcome was the same, my father would order my mother about in low, demanding tones, beat her, or hold her down, but no matter the treatment, she clearly loved it.

Apparently, that was the way sex was done. Now I knew the method my interest in getting a girlfriend was definitely growing, as was my libido.

NINE – STELLA

After our first great night together – who was I kidding? It hadn't just been great, it had been body-melting, mind-blowing, exceptional stuff – Nathan didn't touch me again sexually for well over a month, much to my complete frustration. A whole frigging month! Instead, the following week when I arrived for my first full weekend with him he explained that we needed to go through a brief period of non-sexual training to build our trust, an explanation I couldn't help but meet with a petulant frown.

I was horny as hell and yet he was set on denying me. Wasn't he horny too? Since last weekend's amazing sex I'd struggled to think of anything apart from getting into bed with Nathan again, but with his reluctance my doubts started to grow, perhaps he didn't feel the same way? Had he changed his mind about our agreement?

Seeing my fractious look Nathan's lips twitched, he seemed to be trying to withhold a smile, *bastard*, but he did at least have the decency to try and explain his thinking. 'For the things we are going to do together you will need to trust me implicitly, Stella, otherwise you won't be able to relax and get the full potential from the experiences.'

Blushing considerably, I nodded my understanding and began to wonder just what type of training the inexplicably sexy Nathan had in store for me. Standing this close to him, his sheer magnetism was just impossible to ignore and I found myself wanting to move nearer to him, even though ironically the idea of being in closer proximity to his raw sexual intensity completely terrified me.

As stupid as it was, the thought that Nathan might be

avoiding sex because he'd changed his mind just wouldn't leave my brain and in the end, I couldn't help voicing my fears. 'Aren't you horny, though?' I asked in a humiliatingly needy tone. God I was pathetic.

The hot, lusty, downright illegal look that crossed Nathan's face was all the answer I needed and almost had my knees buckling under me. Blimey, he could be intensely sexy when he turned it on.

'I am, Stella, you have no idea how much I want to take you again. Repeatedly,' he added darkly making me lick my suddenly dry lips. Allowing a short pause where I thought my brain might short circuit, he then flashed me another promising smile before adding, 'But if you don't relax and enjoy the things we do together then neither will I, which is simply unacceptable, therefore I'm afraid I must insist on training beforehand.' *Wow*, OK then, when he put it that way I suppose training would be OK.

I didn't have to wait long to find out what types of things Nathan had in store for me because just then he produced a black velvet sash from his pocket and passed it to me. Frowning I ran it through my fingers – the material was soft and smooth and somehow erotic to touch, making me quiver. 'To quickly build your trust in me you will spend the majority of this weekend blindfolded and completely reliant on me. Fasten the sash around your eyes,' he instructed swiftly.

What? Spend the weekend blindfolded? I'd only met this guy last weekend, could I seriously do that? Visibly shaking I opened up the blindfold and with wide eyes dared to make eye contact with Nathan to check if his motives looked sincere. My gaze must have shown my obvious hesitancy because Nathan ran the backs of his knuckles down my cheek softly in a reassuring gesture that sent tingles scattering across my skin.

'I'll find it a huge turn-on if you trust me enough to blindfold yourself,' he explained huskily. 'And you can trust me Stella, I promise you that,' he added, his tone low and lusty and oh so sexy. Knowing that I had the power to affect him so much boosted my confidence slightly and so with a nervous swallow I lifted the soft material to my eyes and fastened it behind my head.

It blocked my sight completely. I'd thought I might be able to tie it so that I could peek out the bottom like I had as a kid when we'd played pin the tail on the donkey, or at least have a little light coming in, but the soft flexible material moulded to my face, cutting off all light.

The darkness was too much, I didn't like the sensation one little bit. *Bloody hell*, suddenly I felt overwhelmingly claustrophobic and began to panic slightly, I couldn't breathe … my lungs were too tight, my breaths coming short and sharp, and beads of sweat had started to form on the back of my neck as my hands rose and started to scrabble to untie the knot.

The next thing I knew my hands were pulled down, leaving me still blindfolded, but being cradled in two strong arms and I instinctively buried my head in Nathan's chest and clung to him as I tried to calm my erratic breathing. 'Shhh … it's OK, Stella, I'm here, I'll keep you safe,' he murmured against my hair, his breath warm against my scalp and his touch infinitely reassuring.

This was crazy, I barely knew him, but Nathan's words were ridiculously consoling to me and I felt myself relax immediately, air finding my lungs and soothing me just as his touch was. Somehow, I just knew that he was telling the truth, he might appear stern and unapproachable, but I intrinsically knew Nathan wouldn't let any harm come to me. Besides, being in his arms felt so damn good that I stopped worrying about my lack of sight and instead focused on getting a sneaky feel of his chest.

The rest of my weekend passed mostly in blindfolded darkness. The only times I was permitted to remove it was when I was using the toilet or sleeping, and with the latter I was instructed to set a morning alarm and be blindfolded ready for Nathan to come to my room for 8.30 a.m. Apart from that Nathan guided me around his apartment, fed me, fetched me drinks and even more intimately, undressed me and silently washed me in the shower. This last scenario happened on both mornings and did nothing to quell my horniness, but even though Nathan was clearly just as aroused by it as me – even blindfolded I had felt his jutting erection brush against me several times – he did nothing but bathe and dry me. It was a little weird just how thorough he was with the washing part, actually, cleaning every single part of me and even scraping under my fingernails. I'd never felt quite so clean or well cared for.

As well as general tasks, Nathan also instructed me in the behaviours I should exhibit as his submissive, and patiently explained the things that would incur his punishments. He was so calm and kind that I couldn't really believe it was the same intensely guarded man that I'd had the meeting with last weekend.

I couldn't help but wonder if the presence of my blindfold, and thus my inability to make eye contact, had relaxed Nathan, but whatever it was that had caused his calmer nature I certainly found myself growing to quickly trust him and greatly enjoy our time together, and soon enough I was following his instructions without hesitation even in my blindfolded state.

The only hiccup that first weekend was on the Sunday night when Nathan asked me to allow myself to fall backwards into his waiting arms. It's one of the ultimate tests of trust and used in stupid team-building exercises worldwide, isn't it, but could I do it? No. Perhaps it was the disorientated feeling that the blindfold gave me, or maybe because the trust between us was still too new and fragile, but I couldn't help but step back and save myself as I tried repeatedly to fall without fear.

My disappointing failure at this simple activity was the official end to my first weekend with Nathan. Steadying my shoulders after yet another unsuccessful attempt Nathan swiftly removed the blindfold and I blinked several times to help my eyes adjust to the light flooding back in.

Even though I'd been with him all weekend, it seemed strange to actually *see* Nathan. Gosh, he was so handsome that my knees suddenly felt a bit weak. Unfortunately the novelty of seeing his glorious features was soon forgotten when I saw the frowned look of disappointment on his face at my failure of his final test.

'I'm sorry … Sir,' I muttered, adding his title just to try and make up for not being able to follow his last simple instruction.

'We will try again next week,' Nathan replied curtly in a cool tone, his easy going demeanour seeming to have vanished along with the blindfold. Back to square one again then, I sighed heavily, disappointed that my gentle and caring man from the weekend had vanished so abruptly.

'When you can do it we can move the relationship to the next level.' His tone didn't give away any emotion what so ever, but clearly, his words were meant as a carrot on a stick and I immediately translated them to "as soon as you can do it, we can have sex".

Damn it! Why hadn't I just fallen back into his sodding arms? Then we might very well be having amazing sex right now instead of standing here awkwardly avoiding eye contact like two horny strangers. Well I didn't know about Nathan's state of arousal, but the heavy throbbing between my legs left me in little doubt that I was keyed up and ready to go.

That night as Nathan dropped me at home he parked the car outside my flat, turned to me and handed me a package about the size of a box of tissues that was wrapped in brown paper and tied neatly with parcel string. How curious. I glanced at him but his face was inscrutable, his stoic mask well and truly back in place. Given the nature of our relationship, I certainly hadn't been expecting gifts from him, that was for sure. Licking my lips nervously I gave the parcel a confused look as Nathan began to explain.

'I know you were probably expecting vastly different things from this weekend, Stella, but I appreciate your understanding that we need to build our trust first.' Nathan paused and briefly glanced at me, his strong features looking stark and ominous in the moonlight. 'You may be feeling slightly frustrated, but hopefully this package will ease that. There is a note inside, I expect you to follow my instructions to the letter.' The look he gave me left little doubt that he meant what he said and it was all I could do to get out a whispered, 'Yes, Sir,' as I fled from his car. How ironic, I'd been the one to insist that I only called him Sir in the bedroom, but that was twice now that I'd opted to use it because I found him so bloody intimidating!

Almost as soon as I was through the door to my apartment, I was tearing into the package all the while knowing that I was exhibiting a complete lack of self-control that super cool Nathan would no doubt loathe.

Oh my God. A nervous giggle escaped my throat as I ripped the lid off the box only to uncover a large flesh-coloured vibrator nestled in pink tissue paper, sat on top of a white card. My eyes widened and I chewed on my lip as I examined it. I had never owned a vibrator before, I'd always wanted to, but had been too embarrassed to walk into a shop and just buy one. Now it seemed I had a man, my new dominant none the less, to do the purchasing for me. Blimey, it was massive. Blushing furiously at the sight of it I reached for the card trying to ignore the silky feel of the vibrators material as I moved it to the side.

Written in elegant and obviously male handwriting I read the note once, sucked in a shocked breath, and then quickly read it again.

Stella,

I trust this gift will relive any sexual frustration you may be feeling after our sexless training weekend. My instructions for your use of this toy are simple, I demand that as you push it in your wet, quivering body you think of me buried to the hilt deep inside you, making you come so fucking hard that you scream for me to never stop.

N

P.S. This toy is to be returned to me when we start a more intimate relationship, once we are sleeping together I will be the only one to make you climax.

Well, he certainly had a way with words didn't he! Choking back a cough at his bluntness, I couldn't help reading it again with wide eyes, imagining Nathan's low lusty voice whispering the words in my ear. Good God. I was suddenly really hot and just in the process of using the card to fan my burning face when Kenny came waltzing into the kitchen with an empty wineglass in his hand.

It vaguely occurred to me that he'd obviously decided to exchange his vegetable liquid diet for another type of liquid altogether, and if I hadn't been so shell-shocked about the vibrator in my hand I would have taken great pleasure in pointing it out to him.

'Hey babes! I didn't hear you get in!' Kenny chorused as he made his way to the fridge for a top up while I frantically shoved the giant dildo back in the box and rammed the lid on to hide it.

'Wine?' He asked, leaning round the fridge door and holding up a bottle of my favourite Pinot Grigio causing me to nod silently. Yes, a cold glass of wine would be good right now; it might cool my raging libido a bit. Although given just how horny I was that was somewhat doubtful, I'd need hosing down with a lake's worth of ice water to calm me down at this rate.

Luckily Kenny seemed oblivious to my lusty silence and set about pouring our drinks while I quickly read Nathan's card again, taking a slightly ragged breath as I imagined him writing it with the vibrator sat on his desk and a dark smile on his face. My legs suddenly felt very wobbly. Dumping my bag down I gripped the edge of the breakfast bar and realised that my body was practically on the brink of an orgasm from just reading Nathan's note. I rolled my eyes. God only knows what I'd be like when we finally had sex again.

TEN - NATHAN

It wasn't long after my perverse discovery of my parents' unorthodox sexual tastes that the shit had really hit the fan in the Jackson household. I was 18 by this point and my brother Nicholas was fast approaching his 16th birthday, but still our father's dominant treatment of our whole family continued.

It had been on Nicholas' actual birthday that 'it' had happened. I had been in my room waiting for my nightly punishment visit from my father, as expected my door opened at a little past eight o'clock, but my father didn't come in the room as usual; instead he had leant on the door frame casually, which had immediately set alarm bells ringing for me. 'You can have a night off for good behaviour, son.' my father had said lightly, but my stomach immediately tensed, I never got nights off, apart from Sundays that was, so this was definitely unexpected. 'I'm taking your mother out with some work colleagues shortly, but as your brother is officially 16 today I thought I'd give him a welcome to adulthood before I go out.'

It had been the same when I had turned 16. Once my masculinity had kicked in with me growing taller in stature and broader in muscles, my father's beatings had increased in strength and duration. Almost as if he was proving that no matter how big or strong his sons would grow he would always be the one in control of us.

For a good 20 minutes that night, I had to lie on my bed and listen to the aggressive grunts of my father as he repeatedly hit Nicholas with God knows what implement in the room next door. To his credit, Nicholas only cried out twice, probably on the first two blows, but after that, my brother had remained painfully silent.

Finally, I heard the click of my brother's door closing and my father's footsteps passing my door on the way to the master bedroom. The noises of my mother and father changing and moving downstairs went on for a further half an hour or so until finally I heard them leave the house at a little past nine o'clock. Waiting for at least ten minutes to make sure they were definitely not returning I then crept from my room to check on Nicholas.

The sight that met me turned my blood cold and caused me to instantly drop to my knees in shock. Curled on the floor in the foetal position was Nicholas, his hands tied to the radiator and his entire torso covered in long, angry welts and bluing bruises. A cane was tossed casually on the bed, but it was neither of these sights that shocked me into crying for the first time in years. No, it was my brother's deathly pale face and the deep red blood pooling around Nicholas' slashed wrist that broke me.

The scissors that my brother had obviously used to cut his own wrist lay discarded next to his bloodied body and I used the exact same scissors, slippery with his blood, to cut Nicholas' unresponsive arm from its restraints before hurriedly tying a makeshift bandage around the wound, scooping him up and carrying him downstairs to my mother's car. I didn't care that I hadn't passed my driving test because my father hadn't allowed me to take any lessons, I'd be damned if I was wasting precious minutes waiting for an ambulance when my brother was bleeding out in my arms, so I climbed in the car and did what I'd watched my mother do a thousand times.

Ignition, clutch, gear, accelerate.

Miraculously it worked, after several juddering gear changes and a near miss at a junction I had an unconscious Nicholas in hospital within eight minutes.

Our father never beat us again after that night. In fact, our father would never see us again after that night, because the police had picked our parents up as soon as they arrived home and taken them directly to the police station.

For reasons I couldn't fully explain I had always had a grudging respect for my father and initially this had made me reluctant to admit everything to the doctors and policemen that fought to save my brother that night. But when Nicholas came around and looked at me with such complete desolation in his eyes I had known there was nothing else for it, I couldn't allow my brother to suffer any longer.

The whole story was told. My parents were arrested, my father for child abuse, and my mother as an accessory and that was it, the Jackson brothers were now alone in the world. Nicholas was 16, technically able to go his own way, but because the psychiatrist that treated him deemed him to be a 'vulnerable young person' it was decided that he would be put up for fostering whilst he stabilised.

My brother was everything to me, so there was no fucking way I was letting him go and live with strangers. I immediately applied for, and was eventually granted, guardianship over him until he reached 18. Some social worker busy body told me I could claim benefits to get us a little cash each week, but I wasn't going to rely on anyone else anymore. I was in control now. Not some prick in the benefits office, and not my father. I was the man of the house now.

By the end of the following week I was no longer a college student, I was full-time guardian to a 16-year-old boy, my broken and fragile brother, and had managed to get myself a job as a labourer for a local building contractor.

ELEVEN – STELLA

Unfortunately, even with Nathan's veiled promise that we would have sex once I fully trusted him, I still found my stubborn body unable to give up its fear and I repeatedly failed the test of falling back into his arms. He would only ever attempt the exercise after a full weekend together just before I was due to leave, but if I was unsuccessful again today, this would be week five of my failure. Not to mention week five of no sex and week five of frigging frustration. At this rate, my new vibrator would need the batteries replacing sooner rather than later.

Still, Nathan had stuck to his guns and made no move on me sexually; our days together had been spent in much the same way as the first weekend. Even with my final failures I knew I was definitely more comfortable in his presence now, so although frustrating, his training was at least working.

As I waited for him in the lounge, blindfolded, it suddenly occurred to me that actually, when I thought about it, this was probably the most intimate I'd ever been with any man in my entire life. Which was ironic really, seeing as we weren't even sleeping together. Nathan had literally been catering for my every need, and although he didn't speak that often apart from his instructions, the closeness I felt when he was washing me in the shower, or combing and drying my hair afterwards, was exceptional. As corny as it sounds, it was almost as if words weren't necessary between us.

The carpet must have muffled his footsteps because the next second I felt a hand touch my shoulder to alert me of Nathan's presence. My skin jumped to alertness as it always did when he was near, then his hand dropped away and I felt Nathan lean in behind me lowering his mouth close to the sensitive skin below my ear. 'On the count of three, fall backwards, Stella.' But this week he added an extra statement. 'You know you can trust me to catch you,' he urged me. His breath was warm on my neck and sent a tingle across my skin and just like that I knew without a doubt that he would catch me, Nathan *would* keep me safe. This time when Nathan counted to three I let out a soft gasp, opened my arms wide, and merely fell as if sinking back onto a huge feather-filled mattress.

Not only did Nathan catch me in his strong arms as he had promised, but he then wasted no time in scooping me up with a growl, turning me in his arms and kissing me hungrily. *At last.* But unfortunately, his lips rose from mine far too quickly for my liking as he pulled away and removed the blindfold to reveal his flushed face and glittering eyes. 'Get plenty of rest this week, Stella, you're going to need your energy next weekend,' he said huskily. 'When you arrive here next Friday you better be prepared to hand yourself over to me completely. Bring back the vibrator too, there will be no more need for it, it's going to be me driving you wild from now on,' he promised darkly as he escorted me and my quivering body to his car.

86

TWELVE – NATHAN

Several months had passed since the hideous night when Nicholas had tried to kill himself, regardless of time passing I still occasionally found the events playing through my mind. It was a more frequent occurrence for my poor damaged brother, however, and I was often woken by Nicholas' screams when feverish nightmares took hold of him in the dark hours around midnight.

There were certain visual similarities between my father and me. I knew that, what with our impressive stature, icy blue eyes, and blond hair, but sometimes Nicholas would look up at me with apprehension and say, 'You look just like Father when you do that, Nathan, I don't like it.' So for the sake of my brothers mental health I had grown my hair slightly longer to adjust my appearance and would always quickly change whatever behaviour it was that upset Nicholas. Deep down, however, I couldn't move my belief system away from the fact that my father had taught me the correct way to behave in life.

When I finally got up the courage to ask a girl at my work out I hadn't really known what to do, so when she invited me in to her place for a coffee I did just what my father would have done and bossed her about. She hadn't liked this one little bit, not like my mother had seemed to, so I'd tried demanding a kiss instead, wondering if perhaps that was what she wanted. It wasn't, she'd thrown me out and told me to 'Get yourself a sub if you want to be so fucking bossy.'

Those words were what had led me to David Halton at Club Twist. Having gone home after my failed date I had immediately looked up what a 'sub' was, and apart from finding various entries about American sandwiches I had finally discovered a variety of sites devoted to submissive men and women who loved to be controlled in all manner of situations. When I'd searched more specifically for submissives in the London area a link for Club Twist came up and not long after my first visit to see David Halton, Nathan the dominant was born.

THIRTEEN – STELLA

What a week! With Nathan's intense promises last Sunday about the things that lay ahead for me I had barely been able to concentrate on work at all. Instead, my mind had been on Nathan's contract, Nathan's sublime kissing, and Nathan's amazing body ... but if I'm honest then I'll admit that most of my time had been spent on imagining the things Nathan might do *to* me and *with* me.

I'd been so 'Nathan-focused' at work that during one of my lulls in concentration I had made use of my mobile Internet to go online and purchase some rather risqué clothing that made me turn beetroot red as I pressed the 'order' button, but that I hoped Nathan would like. All of this was against office policy of course – '*no phones allowed*' signs were plastered everywhere, and no doubt there was an unwritten rule against using office time to purchase corsets and crotchless panties, but seeing as I pretty much ran the floor I worked on I decided to risk it. Imagining Nathan's reaction to my new purchases when I arrived at his apartment on Friday night made the risk worth it, and was enough to get me so hot and bothered that I'd had to go outside for some fresh air to calm my rampaging libido on several occasions. Perhaps I should start bringing my vibrator to work. Although technically Nathan had banned me from using it now, hadn't he?

But now finally it was Friday! Jeez, last week had felt like a frigging eternity. I'd rushed straight home from work and barely spoken a word of sense to Kenny during dinner, hardly touching the food that he had prepared, but he'd merely eyed me knowingly, removed the pasta from in front of me and forced me to eat a slice of plain toast instead.

Six-thirty rolled around, and at last, I could think about leaving my place to go to Nathan's apartment. Donning my newly purchased outfit, I sprayed myself with my favourite perfume, shrugged on a long coat to cover my skimpy clothing and headed to the lounge where Kenny was waiting for me. Most weeks I'd just got the bus or train to Nathan's home in Docklands, but I hadn't wanted to wear my 'surprise' outfit on public transport tonight so Kenny had offered to drive me over, although I suspected the ulterior motive behind his kindness was his nosy curiosity about where Nathan lived.

Pursing his lips, Kenny eyed my long coat suspiciously as he rubbed his goatee between his finger and thumb and gave me a probing glance. 'Do I want to know what you're wearing under there, Stella?'

'Nope,' was my tart reply, but it was accompanied by a blush so hot that Kenny giggled loudly, his imagination no doubt in overdrive, then with a wink he linked arms with me and escorted me to his car.

No more than 15 minutes later we were outside Nathan's apartment block both standing on the pavement gazing skywards. 'Fuck, does his penthouse cover the entire top floor?' Kenny asked in jealousy-tinged amazement.

'Yep,' I confirmed with a nod. 'He's even got a gym and a cinema room in there.'

'Really?' Kenny's shocked squeal was louder than I had expected and I turned to him with a grin. 'I'm so jealous, Stella, I wish I was banging a billionaire.'

'I doubt he's a billionaire, but sorry, Ken, I'm pretty sure Nathan only digs women,' I joked lightly. At least this banter was helping to calm my leaping nerves.

'Ask him if he has a suitably handsome and equally rich gay brother,' Kenny called as I waved goodbye and made my way inside the foyer. 'Or bisexual!' he yelled, prompting me to roll my eyes and pointedly ignore him. 'I'm not fussy!' he cried desperately as the lift opened in front of me. Wasn't that the truth! Kenny would bed any man as long he showed a vague knowledge of fashion and had a body that was suitably 'bangable', as he put it. Basically, male, under the age of 50, and preferably with blue eyes.

My light moment with Kenny was now gone and I found myself outside the door to Nathan's apartment chewing on my lip and desperately twirling the ring on my thumb. Well, this was it. Placing my weekend bag on the floor I undid the buttons on my jacket, took a deep breath for courage and rang the bell.

FOURTEEN – NATHAN

At about ten minutes to seven, I frowned as my doorbell rang. I'd given Stella a key to my apartment so the bell ringing made no sense to me unless she was ignoring my request to let herself in upon arrival. Perhaps Stella would be receiving her first punishment sooner than I had been expecting, I thought in annoyance as I strutted across the room and harshly pulled open the door with a scowl to match my mood.

'Gift for Mr Jackson.' Stella murmured softly in front of me, then slipping the coat from her shoulders she let it drop to the floor before linking her hands in her submissive pose and turning her flushed face towards the ground.

Holy fucking buckets of shit.

All thoughts of anger and punishment slipped from my brain as my mouth hung open and my gaze took in Stella stood in the hallway – a sight that caused my groin to go rock hard within a matter of seconds. Stella, my supposedly inexperienced submissive, was standing in front of me wearing possibly the most smoking hot outfit I had ever seen. High black leather boots clung to her legs, stopping just below her stockinged knees and the suspenders holding up the stockings she wore were just visible below the short black skirt at her thighs. If possible, the top half was even more stunning, Stella was strapped into a silver corset so tight it sucked her waist to practically nothing, pushing her breasts up and out and was barely covering her nipples with a froth of black and silver lace.

Even with the incredible outfit, my eyes couldn't help but linger on the pale blue collar fastened around her neck. What the hell? My eyebrows flew up, she had bought *herself* a collar? It was about an inch wide, in a colour that was at odds with the blacks and grey of her outfit, but matched her eyes perfectly. Pursing my lips I wondered if Stella knew the significance of the collar she was wearing or if she had merely purchased it to add to her outfit. One thing was for sure, no matter how good she looked in it, or how much the idea of collaring her suddenly appealed to me, there was no way I was going to let her get away with her presumptuous behaviour.

Seeing as she was a novice I decided to deal with the collar issue once Stella was safely inside my apartment. Delaying the moment I ran my gaze over her again. 'You look incredible, Stella,' I murmured thickly. '*Fuck.*' I didn't often swear out loud, but I couldn't help but curse under my breath at just how true my words were.

'I hope we might do, Sir.' Stella replied teasingly causing me to shake my head in complete surprise at her playful confidence. She might not be so confident once I informed her of her gigantic slip with the collar though, I thought with a smirk.

Stepping back to let Stella enter I calmly closed the door all the while feeling how my heart was rampaging under my skin. Perhaps it was time for a countdown? Breathing in through my nose I did my usual five to zero and then feeling marginally more in control I reached out for her. My fingers were magnetically drawn to the soft velvet collar at her neck and as I ran my fingers across it I felt Stella's skin tremble under my touch. It seemed that she was just as affected as me, which pleased me greatly.

'Do you know the symbolism of a collar in a dom/sub relationship Stella, or is this just for decoration?' I questioned thickly.

'It shows I'm yours, Sir. Your property.' Stella murmured softly, a small smile turning up the corner of her mouth and making me want to kiss her there immediately. 'You told me to come prepared to give myself to you … so I did, I'm all yours, Sir.'

Well, fuck me. Stella's response totally blew my mind. The urge to press her against the wall and lay claim to her there and then very nearly overwhelmed me, but the dominant streak in

94

me couldn't get past her mistake in collaring herself and so thankfully I dredged up my reserves of self-control and managed to hold myself back.

I am in control. Or at least I used to be before Stella walked into my life.

FIFTEEN – STELLA

Flashing a brief glance at Nathan before averting my eyes it had been impossible to read the expression on his face. I was fairly sure that he liked my outfit and was turned on like me, but as he stared at the collar on my neck the silence between us stretched on long enough for me to start to worry that I might have done something wrong by wearing it. I'd researched collars carefully, and knew it to be the show of an ultimate commitment in a dominant relationship, although technically I might have gone about it the wrong way by just turning up with it on. Or perhaps he was staring at it because commitment like that wasn't what Nathan wanted from me? Perhaps he just wanted a few weeks of fun. The more I thought about it the more I decided that I'd probably made a huge mistake wearing it. Bugger, I'd only been here 30 seconds and I'd stuffed up already.

Just as I was about to look up and check Nathan's reaction he slipped his fingers under the soft material of the collar and gently tugged. His action took me by surprise and unbalanced me in my high heels so that I ended up staggering forwards into his arms clumsily colliding with his chest.

'Damn right you're mine,' he muttered hoarsely as he hauled me roughly against him and kissed me purposefully, well and truly claiming my mouth with almost bruising ferocity. Then, just as quickly as it had started, Nathan withdrew his lips from mine and stood back leaving me feeling wobbly and cold. 'This, however ...' he stated in an icy tone, running his fingers across my collar again, '... is rather presumptuous of you, Stella.'

Forcing a swallow down my dry throat I flashed a glance at Nathan. His eyes were still fixed on my collar and a deep frown was marring his forehead. That wasn't a good sign, and to top it off, there was even a muscle jumping along his tightly clenched jaw. Shit, he might not be screaming or shouting, but there was no way to miss the fact that he was clearly angry and I felt my skin tingle with trepidation.

'Come with me, Stella.' As Nathan turned and moved away he still had one finger tucked under my collar, so despite his apparent request I really had little choice but to comply as he led me speedily through the lounge towards the kitchen.

Stopping by the central unit in the kitchen Nathan finally removed his finger from my neck. 'Wait here.' He instructed crisply, in the same cold tone of voice that I was quickly coming to dread.

Nathan seemed so angry with me that I hardly dared to move a muscle whilst I waited for him to return – even my breathing was shallow and minimal. When he finally reappeared he stood before me, legs spread and arms crossed over his broad chest in a posture that screamed of authority and almost made me want to curl up into a ball to avoid whatever was about to come my way.

'This,' he ground out as he tapped at my collar again, 'is a problem.' Crossing his arms again he shifted slightly on the spot before continuing. 'I know you're new to this, Stella, but for you to tell me that it shows you are mine indicates that you must have done some research on it, am I right?'

'Yes.' My voice was the tiniest it had ever been.

'Then surely you must have seen that it is the dominant partner who chooses if and when to give a collar?'

I was totally out of my depth here. I knew nothing about this world and yet I'd naively thought this would be a good idea. *Stupid, stupid, stupid girl.* Realising that Nathan was still silently waiting for my response I licked my parched lips and nodded, 'I did see that, but … I … I wanted to please you, and I thought giving myself to you might do that …' I sounded like the clueless idiot I was, so I gave up on my stuttered excuse and just shut my mouth.

'So you merely assumed I would want a more permanent and substantial relationship with you?' he enquired in that horribly distant tone again. Closing my eyes I winced, I had royally fucked this up, and really there was nothing I could say to improve the situation so I just stayed quiet.

After what seemed like an age of silence Nathan spoke again in a softer tone, 'Your reasons and sentiment please me greatly, Stella. I cannot, however, allow you to wear this.'

'I would never even consider collaring someone until I knew if we were compatible or not. However, the idea of you wearing my collar is rather alluring, so I am willing to compromise slightly in this. I will replace your collar with a simple one of my own; consider it a training collar if you like. This in turn shall be replaced at a later date with a more decorative and permanent one if I see fit.'

Reaching to the side of me Nathan opened a drawer and rummaged through the contents. Frowning, I wondered what on earth he could want, but then my frown quickly turned to an expression of shock when he withdrew a pair of scissors and held them up. 'Hold very still.' He commanded, before leaning in and pressing the cool metal of the blade to the quivering skin of my neck. One simple snip later and the ruined strip of beautiful velvet fluttered uselessly to the ground by my feet.

His unnecessarily harsh actions caused my eyebrows to practically rise out of my forehead. How dare he? 'I …' But my sentence was cut off by Nathan as he leaned in next to my ear. 'Collaring yourself is a serious misconduct, Stella, with many doms your punishment would have been very severe. Seeing as you are new to this I chose to make my point in a different way by cutting it off. If you would rather my punishment was more standard I'm sure I could arrange that for you.' He paused for a fraction of a second to let his words sink in. 'Did you still have something to say?' he then enquired mildly. His mere mention of the word 'punishment' had me snapping my teeth shut and rapidly shaking my head.

'Good girl.' Then reaching into his pocket Nathan withdrew a simple strip of dark leather and held it up in front of me. 'Your replacement.' He commented as he leaned in to place it around my neck.

This time I really couldn't hold back my thoughts, 'But it's nowhere near as pretty as …' But the challenging expression on

Nathan's face as he tilted my chin back and glared at me stopped me in my tracks. I really needed to install a mouth filter and shut the hell up.

'Nowhere near as pretty as the one you bought?' he demanded, 'We've barely spent any time together intimately, Stella, how do I know if you deserve to wear a pretty collar?' Licking my lips nervously I decided his question was probably rhetorical, so stayed quiet. 'Like I said before, if things between us develop pleasingly then I *may* consider giving you something different. Until then you wear this whenever you are with me.'

Fastening the collar behind my neck Nathan stood back and assessed it with a small smile that was somehow both arrogant and appealing all at once. 'Have I been clear, or do you need me to explain my actions further?'

As I stood before Nathan's looming figure I felt very much like a chastised school girl, but I had at least learnt my lesson without getting any sort of actual punishment so I shook my head. 'No, I understand.' I really should have known better when I'd researched it all, so biting my lip I also decided to add an apology, 'I'm sorry Sir, I hope I haven't spoilt our first proper night together.'

Cupping my face Nathan tilted it upwards and graced me with a second of actual eye contact. 'Not at all. Now that little issue has been dealt with, we can get tonight back on track.' he muttered as his hands slipped to my waist, gripped my hips and practically swooped down to kiss me. His lips were hot and hard against mine and it was all I could do to cling to Nathan when his tongue demanded entry to my mouth at the same time as he scooped me up and carried me towards the bedroom that was my space within his apartment.

Depositing me onto a wooden upright chair Nathan gripped my chin and forcefully tilted my mouth up for another scorching kiss. 'My intention tonight had been to get you naked as quickly as possible, Stella, but seeing as you have taken such great effort over your outfit I think we will leave you dressed for a while longer so I can fully appreciate it. I will however ask you to remove your underwear.'

Oh. Blushing as bright as a flame, I raised my wide eyes to

Nathan and licked my lips nervously again. If I kept on like this they'd be so chapped I'd need an entire tub of lip balm to repair them. His eyes were glittering as he briefly met my gaze, before lifting an eyebrow curiously. 'I take it from your expression that you're not wearing any underwear tonight, are you, Stella?' Swallowing loudly I was about to nod my answer, but Nathan beat me to it by leaning down and casually flicking the hem of my skirt up. I felt a brush of air on my heated skin and watched as Nathan sucked in a breath through flared nostrils. His suspicions must have been confirmed by a flash of my nude, pink pussy. This was the very valid reason that I hadn't wanted to arrive by public transport tonight.

'My, my, you are a naughty little submissive, aren't you?' he chided almost playfully, but no, this was No-Nonsense-Collar-Cutting-Nathan speaking, so surely in my highly aroused state I must just have misread his light-hearted comment.

Nathan walked behind me and my ears pricked as I heard him open one of the wooden drawers that stood in the corner of the room. The top four drawers held the clothes I left here for the weekends, but not the bottom drawer. When I had looked in the bottom drawer on my very first weekend, I'd seen such a wide range of sex toys that I had blushed furiously and immediately slammed the drawer shut. Like a true coward I'd deliberately avoided looking ever since, but now as Nathan dug around in the drawer I was wishing that I had inspected the contents with a little more care to prepare myself for what was to come.

By this point, my heart was hammering so hard in my chest that I felt sure Nathan must be able to hear it. Nervous anticipation was making me start to get a bit clammy behind my neck and after Nathan's quick inspection between my legs, I suspected I was getting pretty damp down there too. After noises of rummaging that sent my imagination running wild, I finally heard a hum of approval from Nathan followed by the soft click of the drawer closing again. He'd chosen.

'Arms behind your back,' Nathan ordered in a low tone next to my ear, sending goosebumps rising on my skin. Since being with Nathan I'd discovered just what an erogenous zone my ear was, just one hot, whispered breath on that area was enough to have me quivering at his feet. Mind you, I pretty much did that anyway just from the sight of him.

An involuntary shiver ran through my body, from fear or anticipation I wasn't sure, but my weeks of training ensured that I responded to his orders without hesitation, dropping my arms to the side of the chair and holding them back behind myself.

The touch of Nathan's skin caressing the pulse point on my wrist made me gasp, but a frisson of panic ran up my spine as I felt a cold bracelet close around one wrist and then quickly around the other with a loud clicking noise. Drawing in a shocked breath, I closed my eyes as recognition hit me. *Handcuffs*.

Nathan had cuffed my hands behind my back. When I tried to move my arms, I realised that as well as cuffing my wrists together he had looped the chain of the cuffs through the wooden rails on the back of the chair effectively stopping me from standing up. Pervy *and* cunning, what a combination.

Calming my raging heartbeat was near impossible, it was literally galloping against my ribs, but I tried to repeatedly remind myself that Nathan wouldn't harm me, if I'd learnt anything in our weeks of training it was that I could trust him, no matter how scary he might seem, or how daunting the situation might be at the moment, Nathan had proved to me that he was trustworthy. *I hoped*.

Nathan chose that moment to lazily stroll around in front of me with a wicked gleam in his eye and two silk scarves hanging loosely from one hand. My mind was too overwhelmed to concentrate on anything other than their colour, blood red. Without a word, he bent in front of me and tied my ankles to either leg of the chair spreading my feet, knees, and thighs wide apart, but restraining me from moving my limbs fully.

Standing back, Nathan ran a hand across his jaw and an appraising gaze across my seated form before a frown spread across his handsome brows. God, what had I done wrong now? But before I could try to work out what was wrong Nathan stepped forwards and after placing a short, hard kiss on my lips he gripped my hips and with slight difficulty lifted me, pushed my skirt several inches up my thighs and then shifted me forwards on the seat so I was sat right on the edge.

Moving back again Nathan reassessed me and grinned broadly, a look so stunning that it made me forget my nerves as a lusty breath caught in my throat. 'Now there's a perfect view,' Nathan murmured salaciously. I was well aware that now my legs were spread Nathan would be able to see right up my bunched skirt to the apex of my thighs, an area of my body now beyond my control, which seemed to be getting hotter and wetter by the second.

Letting out a low growl of approval Nathan stalked forwards again and ran a finger gently from my left temple across my cheek, over my jaw and down my neck to where it lingered on my collarbone leaving a hot trail of needy skin in its wake.

Chuckling at my groan of pleasure Nathan brushed my bottom lip with his thumb before lowering his head for a kiss. I had expected a forceful barrage like Nathan's previous two kisses, but to my surprise, he brushed his lips across mine so lightly that at first I thought I had imagined it. Repeating the gesture Nathan buried a hand in my hair and gently tilted my head up to deepen his kiss by pushing his tongue between my parted lips to leisurely explore my mouth.

If I hadn't been tied to the chair, it was quite possible that I would have fallen right off it from the dizzying sensations spreading through my body from his heady kisses. With his free hand Nathan skilfully flicked the top of my corset down to reveal my breasts, my nipples already erect from arousal and apparently too tempting for Nathan to resist as his lips suddenly shifted from my mouth to trail across my skin until he finally sucked one nipple into his mouth and laved the hard bud with his tongue, causing me to cry out needily and buck in my chair.

Given the limited movement I had I began to writhe shamelessly in my restraints as his ministrations shifted to my other breast, but that was nothing compared to the delicious sensations that swept through my body as one of Nathan's hands finally slipped between my parted legs. After only seconds of teasing my wet lips, Nathan's fingers slid up my folds to the sensitive nub that was screaming for his attention and he began lazily circling it and driving me wild with sensation.

I was so turned on and sensitive that it almost hurt, and as much as I found it hard to believe, I felt myself slipping towards an orgasm almost as soon as Nathan had touched me. I knew he had serious amounts of sex appeal, but I had never, *never* in my life managed to achieve a climax from anything other than missionary position, let alone from a man's hand, so I hadn't expected this to be any different. But after mere moments of Nathan's skilled touch I felt my abdomen begin to tighten with my approaching orgasm.

'Come for me, Stella.' He murmured against my mouth and as if on cue I arched my back and let out a moan that verged on a whimper as a climax smashed over me, my body pulsating so hard it was almost painful. He hadn't even needed to put a finger inside me for goodness sake!

Wow. *Just wow*. That had been *in-cred-ib-le*, but before I had a chance to voice this fact or even briefly start recovering, Nathan dropped to his knees in front of me and replaced his fingers with his tongue which immediately began to lick along my folds and run circles around my swollen clitoris, making my body weep with moisture all over again. Christ, this man was good.

The feeling of his hot probing tongue on my already over-sensitive clit was just too much to take and my head began to swim hazily. 'Oh God … Nathan … *Sir*, I can't …' I begged haphazardly, seriously doubting my ability to stay conscious if Nathan chose to give me another amazing orgasm like the one I had just experienced.

In response Nathan merely chuckled against my quivering flesh, which in itself sent vibrations seeping through my already over-sensitised skin, but he made no effort to move away. In fact, if anything he doubled his endeavours plunging first one and then two fingers into my moist depths making me cry out from the deliciousness running through my body. 'You can, and you will.' Nathan ordered, his words vibrating through me as he spoke. Holy fuck, this guy had serious skills in the sex department.

Nathan increased the pressure of his tongue and the speed of his fingers until unbelievably I felt my body tensing again towards a second peak. This felt so good it was like Nathan was introducing me to a whole new reality of pleasure. Sensing my imminent release Nathan did a quick swap, moving his thumb to my clitoris and plunging his tongue right inside my tight channel, causing me to shriek embarrassingly and then shamelessly thrust my hips up against his face as I came hard around his lapping tongue and screamed my release though heaving sobs.

Completely exhausted by the earth-shattering start to my weekend, my head rolled to the side as I struggled against the sudden tiredness that swept through my entire body. Crikey, no wonder Nathan had a gym in his apartment; he'd need it to keep up his fitness and stamina if this type of sex was usual for him.

As I was left feeling floaty and groggy Nathan seemed completely calm as he speedily removed my bindings and cuffs before spending several minutes gently massaging my wrists and ankles where the cuffs and scarves had been. Then, scooping me up he carried me to the bed where he laid me out and thankfully allowed me to relax momentarily while he stripped us both of our clothing.

Even in my exhausted and disorientated state I wasn't allowed to rest for long though, and over the next two hours Nathan continued to bombard me with his incredible sexual prowess in a variety of different positions and opening my eyes to the astounding new world of sex that I could expect during my time with him.

I quite literally had never known it could be *this* good.

Surprisingly I found calling Nathan 'Sir' during our session wasn't a problem at all, in fact he was so in control and compelling that it had just felt natural to me.

I had, however, earned one brief punishment, a swift spanking, after I forgot myself and gazed into Nathan's eyes for what he obviously deemed to be too long. Much to my surprise, I had enjoyed even this aspect of the evening, probably because Nathan had followed it up with such a deliciously fast orgasm for me that the mild pain of the spanking was soon forgotten.

Something about the stinging slaps had been incredibly arousing for me though, and now as I lay there in my post-coital afterglow I wasn't entirely sure how to feel about that – did it make me some kind of freak?

It wasn't my most elegant pose, but I was currently sprawled across the bed on my stomach completely naked and seriously struggling to keep my eyes open. I was so tired I felt like I could sleep for a week. Apparently, Nathan had finally had his fill for the night and after gently cleaning me with a damp washcloth he had disappeared into the bathroom where he had been showering for an absolute age. He seemed to be just as thorough with his own hygiene as he had been with mine when he washed me. Mind you, I didn't really give a hoot about his odd washing habits when he was as good in bed as he was! If tonight's performance was anything to go by then the word insatiable really didn't begin to describe him.

Giving in to the temptation to close my eyes I felt the mattress dip as Nathan finally returned from the bathroom and sat on the edge of the bed. He was silent for several moments but I was just too shattered to open my eyes.

'So Stella, with regards to your inability to climax … was this issue present tonight?' he enquired mildly. A smile broke on my lips even though my eyes stayed shut, I was just too exhausted to try and re-open them, too deliciously sated from the mind blowing sex session. Even with my eyes closed, the smugness in Nathan's tone was easily detectable and I was fairly certain that if I looked he'd be smirking darkly.

'No, Sir,' I replied with a contented sigh that verged on a delirious giggle. I really was *that* exhausted.

'How many times did you come?' he demanded next, although I guessed from his tone that he already knew the answer.

'I gave up counting after number three, Sir,' I admitted, a lazy grin spreading across my bruised lips. In truth, I'd lost count as time slowed down and one delicious toe curling climax had blurred with the next. Until today I hadn't even thought that was possible.

Lost count! I giggled again. I had never dreamed I would be able to use those words in relation to my own body and an orgasm total.

'It was at least five, although after I spanked you and took you from behind it felt quite like you came twice in quick succession, so perhaps six,' Nathan stated informatively. 'I believe you had referred to your previous inability to climax as your "peculiarity". I hope I've proved there is nothing at all peculiar about you, Stella.'

'Yes, Sir.' Stretching my blissfully achy body, I rolled beneath the sheets and tugged the duvet around myself to form a cocoon. 'Or perhaps it's just you, Sir,' I mumbled softly. 'Clearly up until now I've been sleeping with the wrong men. Least I've rectified that,' I murmured drowsily before a deep breath escaped my lips indicating that sleep was finally claiming me.

SIXTEEN – NATHAN

With her eyes closed as she drifted deeper in her sleep Stella didn't see the satisfied smile that slipped onto my lips at her complimentary words, nor did she witness the possessive way that I gazed at her as she began to doze. That was definitely something to be done when no one was watching.

Once she was soundly asleep, I allowed myself to crawl below the covers and curl protectively around Stella's back feeling a deep satisfaction sweep through me that I hadn't felt for a very long time. If ever.

The sex this evening had been incredible, more than incredible, and now that Stella had finally built up her trust in me I was surprised by just how euphoric I had been left feeling. Almost like I imagined it might feel if I were experiencing a particularly good high on drugs. Not that I'd ever experimented with drugs – too much risk of losing control, something I would never do. Control was everything to me, had been for such a long time now.

As I allowed myself half an hour wrapped around Stella's soft sleeping body, I thought back to how this first night with Stella was literally a million miles away from my first ever attempts at sex. An ironic smile curled my lips as I thought again of how David Halton in Club Twist had arranged for me to meet with a submissive for the first time, Louisa, she'd been called.

Using the example set by my father I had probably been too violent with her really, but thankfully as luck turned out Louisa had been a bit of a masochist and had loved it. Reluctantly I had to give David Halton the credit for this; I have long suspected that he had had me figured out right from the start and deliberately selected Louisa and her love of pain to be my first. Clever man.

At the time I had felt an overwhelming confusion swamping my life. My parents were gone, my brother was damaged, and my sex life new and totally bizarre. The upheaval had left me with tumultuous emotions and I'd gotten angry very easily. The rage inside me was just another source of confusion, unsure whether to be annoyed at my father for beating Nicholas, Nicholas for getting my father imprisoned, or myself for not doing something about the whole screwed-up situation earlier. Thank God for David Halton at Club Twist; he might not know when to shut the hell up, but he'd practically saved my life. And God did he have a knack of interviewing new applicants and finding them compatible partners, Louisa couldn't have been a better starting partner for me and now the partnership with Stella was looking like an almost perfect match.

Now, some 13 years after my first experience with Louisa, I was 31 years old and could at last admit that I'd finally burnt out the initial anger that had consumed me for so long, settling myself into a more manageable lifestyle. Control was still important to me, vital really, but the violence that had ruled my father no longer had a hold of my emotions and the punishments I used with my submissives were related to power and pleasure, not pain. I looked down at Stella sleeping beside me and smiled at just how well she'd followed my instructions tonight. She'd been fucking perfect, just as I'd thought.

Not wanting her to think me weak and emotional if I stayed in her room I gave Stella one last lingering gaze and then made myself get up and move to my own cold bed so she would wake up alone tomorrow morning.

SEVENTEEN – STELLA

I woke up grinning. And I'm talking a face-stretching, lips-splitting, eye-crinkling grin. This isn't exactly a usual thing for me, normally when I wake up it's with a yawn, a stretch, or a grimace at just how bloody early it is, but today I was definitely grinning like a Cheshire cat. The cause of my smile? Easy – the delicious dream I'd had last night about Nathan. Ooooh, the things I'd imagined him doing to me!

Rolling over to quench my thirst I suddenly forgot my drink as I realised just how stiff my body was. Sitting up I blinked myself more awake and began experimentally to move my limbs one by one. Interesting. My body was achy and tired in some very unusual places. Some very intimate places.

It took me a while, but my brain finally woke up and allowed me to realise what had happened. *Nathan* – also known as my bad boy, or my sex God – had finally taken me to bed again. Wow, after so long waiting for Nathan and I to have sex I had genuinely thought I'd dreamt it – it certainly wouldn't be the first time I'd had an erotic dream about a certain Mr Jackson – but now as I felt my deliciously achy muscles and the soreness between my legs I realised it had been real.

Very real and *very* good. Flopping backwards, I hugged myself gleefully then glanced around to see if he was still there. Damn, he was gone. A blush spread on my cheeks as I took in the state of the bed with its tangled sheets and no doubt sticky stains hidden amongst the rumpled cotton, but even in my sated state, I couldn't help but feel a pang of disappointment that Nathan was absent.

Reaching across I touched his pillow and found it completely cold, indicating that he had probably been gone for most of the night. Even with all the orgasms he'd given me last night, I would have happily accepted more if I'd woken up and found him next to me, I thought, giggling naughtily.

Biting my lip in satisfaction, I rolled back over and pondered the fact that Nathan had left me sometime in the night and returned to his own room, which was to be expected given our arrangement I suppose, it was hardly like he was my boyfriend was it? More like my sex toy really, or perhaps I was his sex toy … with a giggle I decided that I didn't care who was whose sex toy as long as the action continued in the same way as last night.

Rising from the bed I was about to go directly to the shower when I remembered Nathan's rule about it being my job to clear up the mess we made during sex, so I turned back to the rumpled bed and quickly striped it, piling the sheets by the door to sort out later. Then I showered and dressed in a simple cotton shirt and knee length skirt before getting myself ridiculously nervous about the idea of seeing Nathan. What would it be like today? Would he talk to me or simply disappear into his office and ignore me? All the other weekends that I'd been here I'd been blindfolded so Nathan had sort of been obliged to stay with me, but today was different, like a new start to our time together.

Clicking my tongue I gave myself a sharp talking to, I never let men intimidate me in the business world so I damn well wouldn't let Nathaniel Jackson intimidate me here. Raising my chin, I plucked up my courage and headed out the door to find breakfast, or Nathan, which ever I came across first.

As I approached the kitchen, my nose suddenly locked onto the delicious scent of bacon hanging in the air and my nervousness was forgotten as my stomach gave an embarrassingly loud grumble of approval. Gosh, I hadn't realised how ravenous I was, although given just how much sex I'd had last night it was hardly surprising really, I'd probably burned a week's worth of calories in one go. Making my way down the corridor towards the kitchen the smell grew stronger and my mouth started watering with hunger almost to the point of drooling.

Unfortunately, my drooling only got worse when I actually entered Nathan's stunningly stylish kitchen and my gaze fell upon the man himself.

Oh – my – good – lord.

How the frigging hell had I managed to forget how bloody stunning he was? The beauty of the kitchen paled into insignificance when compared to its owner. Dressed in just a pale blue T-shirt and loose jeans, with bare feet and his hair damp from a shower, Nathan was as casual as I'd ever seen him, but just as breath-taking. Casual definitely suited him, I decided as I slumped against a wall to observe him properly. Mind you, I loved the way he looked in his superbly tailored three-piece suits too.

Fanning my flushed face with my hand I tried to calm my breathing; I was basically panting like an overheated dog. Luckily for me, Nathan was busy at the cooker with his back to me and hadn't noticed me having a mini meltdown in the corner of the room.

By the time he turned to pick up a box of eggs from the counter, I had pretty much got myself under control, which was lucky because Nathan appeared to be rather shocked by my presence and stopped his cooking to stand staring at me.

'Hi,' I murmured, thankful for the support of the wall behind me as Nathan's inscrutable blue gaze continued to bore into me. Well, more specifically he was looking somewhere near my cheek bones, Nathan had rarely made direct eye contact with me last night, and after his statement about disliking it I doubted he ever would.

'Good morning, Stella.' I watched as Nathan's stare ran briefly over me before settling on the leather collar around my neck. I'd taken it off to shower, but when I'd glimpsed it on the dresser as I'd dried myself I'd luckily remembered to put it on again afterwards. I was glad I had now, Nathan wasn't smiling as such, but from the way his gaze lingered there and heated I could tell he was pleased that I was wearing it.

'I didn't hear you come in,' he murmured, his accusing tone almost made me feel a need to apologise for my apparently stealthy entry, but thankfully he changed the subject by indicating to the frying pan with a nod of his chin. 'Hungry?'

I nodded briskly, suddenly so hungry that I was seriously tempted to pinch a rasher of bacon straight from the pan. A smile began to break on my lips as I imagined what Nathan's response would be if I did exactly that, but my thoughts were stopped as he placed down the spatula with a bang and turned to face me crossing his arms across his chest.

'We need to readdress your habit of nodding Stella. It is not an acceptable method of communication for me and frankly I find it extremely disrespectful,' he snapped irritably.

Crikey! He sounded livid and my eyes immediately shot from the sizzling bacon up to his face. Foreboding didn't even get close to describing Nathan's expression, and I gulped nervously. Yep. He was mad. 'Uh … sorry.' I was tempted to add a 'Sir' on to try and soothe him further, but in the stark light of the kitchen, it didn't quite seem right somehow.

'The next time you nod at me I will punish you, Stella. Do you understand?' He threatened in a low voice, but the implications of Nathan's words somehow sent a thrill through me. What exactly would he do to me if I nodded? Was I ready to find out?

Thinking of the act of nodding very nearly made me do it in response to his demand and I had to mentally slap myself back to attention before finally finding my voice. 'Yes, I understand.'

Giving a curt nod of his own, he seemed appeased for the time being. 'Good, come and wash your hands before breakfast.' Wandering over to his side I took a second to inhale his delicious scent and then watched in fascination as Nathan proceeded to give his hands such a thorough scrub it would rival a top heart surgeon.

Handing me a nailbrush, he stood and watched me intently as I also washed my hands, even making me re-do my left one because apparently I'd missed a bit. Wow, he definitely had a thing for cleanliness, didn't he? Not that I was going to say anything after my earlier telling off, no, my plan was to stay quiet this morning and let him take the lead with our new arrangement, but it would certainly be interesting to see how the day panned out.

EIGHTEEN – NATHAN

After spending my entire breakfast wanting to bend Stella over the kitchen counter and spank her enticing little arse for being so bloody distracting, I had now removed myself to the relative peace of my office to get a few hours of work done and try to take my mind off my new tempting submissive. Jesus, she had been just perfect last night, submissive, pliant, and keen, with a sexual appetite that seemed to almost rival mine. God when she'd walked into breakfast still wearing the collar, *my collar,* fuck, it had nearly done me in there and then.

I ran my hands over my face to try and clear my thoughts. For fucks sake, *focus.* Blowing out an exasperated breath I picked up the urgent memo that Gregory, one of my senior directors, had faxed me late last night and rescanned the details of the latest tender that my company had been beaten to. This had happened repeatedly over the last two months, with business getting stolen from under my nose by some mystery firm that was somehow managing to massively undercut my bids.

No matter how many times I read the damn document I just couldn't understand it. By using my own contractors for the builds I'd managed to significantly reduce prices for clients, and I knew for sure that the bid I'd put together had been exceptionally competitive, so how this mystery company had undercut me by a whopping 18 per cent again was beyond me. *Fuck.*

The loss of this one deal wouldn't sink Nathaniel Jackson Architecture, far from it, but it was still fucking irritating and if it carried on then I might start to have some issues. I was the best in the market, how was some untraceable company managing to undercut me? Growling in annoyance I suddenly caught a glimpse of movement in my peripheral vision and glanced up to see Stella standing in the doorway to my office holding a coffee mug in her hand.

Seeing me look her way Stella obviously took my glance as permission to enter because she made her way into the office, placed the mug down on my desk with a small sweet smile and then turned in the direction of the door. I hadn't asked for it, but I had to say the coffee looked perfect – strong with just the correct amount of milk – but at that moment my focus wasn't on the coffee, it was on Stella. She'd headed to the gym to work out after breakfast and had obviously showered since, but was now wearing a tight white tank top, black shorts, and absolutely nothing else if her visible nipples were anything to go by.

Fuck. They weren't just black shorts, I realised with a sharp inhale; they were a pair of my tight Calvin Kleins. Why the sight of Stella wearing a pair of my boxers was so arousing I had no idea, but it was, and below the desk I now found myself rock solid and throbbing. Where the hell had she got them from anyway? Silently cursing her for distracting me from work – *again* – I just couldn't seem to get the thought of Stella's bare pussy rubbing against the inside of the shorts out of my mind. I might have to wear that pair tomorrow.

Suddenly I was consumed with the thought of pushing the infuriating paper work from my desk, spreading Stella out for my display, parting her sweet lower lips and plunging myself into her until she screamed my name. Perhaps I'd remove the boxer shorts and use them to bind her wrists above her head, that'd teach her for being cheeky and borrowing my clothes.

'Stella?' I growled huskily, blinking away my daydream and wondering if I could spend the next ten minutes making it reality. She paused and glanced my way with wide innocent eyes and a small smile that made her look so bloody sexy that I had to bite my lip in an attempt at maintaining my fading self-control.

She was so – fucking – sweet. Too sweet for the likes of me, I thought with a grimace. What she'd done wrong to deserve me I had no idea.

As much as I wanted to take Stella here and now, I debated the temptation and decided that I was way too frustrated with work, not to mention too aroused, to take her and not risk hurting her by being too rough. Especially after all our activities last night, she must be feeling a little sore today and even I wasn't *that* much of an animal, so instead I shook my head. 'Nothing,' I murmured irritably, causing Stella to frown in confusion at my remark as she left the room.

I watched her go, grinding my teeth testily as she finally vanished out of sight before shifting on my seat to relieve the pressure in my damn groin. Then, huffing out a breath I picked up the phone, dialled Gregory's number, and sat back listening to the low hum of the ring tone. Shifting again in my chair I leant forwards for my coffee and realised with a grimace that I hadn't even thanked Stella for the drink, God, I really was the worst kind of arsehole when it came to women and manners.

Once Gregory answered, I didn't bother wasting my breath for an introduction. 'Greg, how the hell have we been undercut again?' I barked harshly. 'Have you found out who this fucking company is yet?'

I heard a heavy sigh down the line from Gregory; apparently, this wasn't how he had planned on spending his Saturday morning. Well tough shit, he was my chief advisor as well as a director and I paid him well enough to answer a few fucking phone calls on a weekend. 'No Nathan, they've somehow made themselves untraceable, all I've found is a post office address and I've got guys on it trying to trace it so we can find an actual person we can speak to. The thing is ...' He paused and I rubbed my forehead in frustration.

'Just fucking spit it out, Gregory,' I muttered, realising that I was swearing out loud far more than usual lately and wondering if that was down to work stress, or Stella stress.

'Well ... it just seems a bit strange that they keep managing to undercut us by the same amount each time, the bids last month were both undercut by exactly 18 per cent too, it's almost like they have an insider in our organisation and they're trying to taunt us.'

Sitting up straighter, I chewed on the inside of my lip as I considered this possibility. It was true, being undercut by exactly 18 per cent each time was too much of a coincidence. 'Look into it, background checks on anyone in the organisation that has access to my office.'

'Will do Nathan,' he agreed immediately before I shut off the phone and slammed it down on my desk.

Twenty minutes after my phone call with Gregory, my rock solid erection had reappeared with a vengeance. Just knowing that Stella and her fuckable little body were somewhere within my apartment had sent my blood pumping down to my cock so hard that it was pretty much making me light headed. For fucks sake, why the hell was I letting Stella affect me so badly? I was never like this over a woman. Someone was stealing business from under my nose – a problem that needed all my focused attention to remedy – but was I thinking about that? No, I was thinking about burying myself balls deep in Stella and fucking her fast and hard to relieve this incessant throb.

Christ, get a grip. Shoving my chair back, I stood up and prowled around my office for several minutes clenching and unclenching my fists. My entire body was tense, I felt like a tightly coiled spring ready to explode at any minute. I briefly considered the idea of having a quick wank to ease my discomfort, but I dismissed it with a scowl, what was I, a fucking randy teenager? Besides, it wouldn't be half as satisfying as a shag with Stella so instead I stalked towards the kitchen to get a coffee to try and distract myself.

After making a drink I moved through to the lounge and stood by the fireplace, putting my coffee on the mantel and gripping the thick marble surface so tightly my knuckles whitened, but at least the stress in my hands seemed to be marginally reducing my raging hard-on.

I had assumed Stella would be tucked away in her room working as she usually was during her free time over the weekend days, but suddenly I felt warm hands settle on my shoulders and my entire body tensed up as my cock sprung straight back to attention. For fuck's sake, I'd only just managed to get control over it! At this moment in time, I was fairly sure that if I clenched my teeth any harder they would shatter into fragments within my skull.

'Not now, Stella,' I managed to growl. Then remembering how I'd been rude to her earlier by not even thanking her for the coffee I begrudgingly gave her a simple explanation. 'I have issues with work that are causing me stress; I just need to be left alone.' Plus I can't get my mind off spreading you wide and pile-driving my raging erection into you, I thought with a grimace, but she was too sweet for me when I felt like this, too innocent, I'd take what I wanted and no doubt hurt her in the process, and as horny as I was right now, even I wasn't depraved enough to do that.

But she ignored me, bloody stubborn woman, and began massaging me more purposefully, rubbing her hands across the hard muscles of my shoulders and working on the tense knots.

'Maybe I can help relax you?' she suggested softly as her hands continued their heavenly work. A moan escaped my throat. Fuck, it felt good. *Too good.* I was barely containing the animal inside me at the moment and with the way I was feeling right now Stella needed to get the hell away from me before I pressed her into the floor and fucked her senseless.

'Stella, I'm not feeling gentle, you need to leave.' The hands that were on my shoulders began to slip lower down my back soothing and rubbing me while simultaneously turning me on even more. Just when I thought I could take no more Stella ran her hands around my hips and cupped my throbbing erection causing a hiss of surprise to break from my lips and making my hips buck wildly. Jesus, I don't think I'd ever felt more tightly wound and desperate for release, in fact I was pretty sure I was going to a burst a blood vessel at any minute, although whether that would be in my pulsing temple or throbbing groin was anyone's guess.

'Maybe I don't want you to be gentle.' Stella purred next to my ear. 'Maybe I like it rough, Sir.' she added salaciously as she gripped me harder and gave a firm squeeze that nearly made me blow on the spot.

Holy shit. Clearly Stella wasn't feeling as innocent as I'd thought, but hearing those words from her mouth was the last straw for me and I spun with a growl, scooping her in my arms before charging in the direction of her bedroom.

Practically throwing Stella onto the bed I was surprised as she immediately crawled off and knelt before me where she began tugging at the zip of my trousers making it perfectly clear that she planned to go down on me.

'Stella, no … I'm too tightly wound for that right now, I'd be too rough with you …' I grated out as she managed to free my straining erection into the cool air of the room where it bobbed about wildly.

Taking me completely by surprise Stella took my hands and placed them on either side of her head. 'I don't mind, use me as you need to, Sir.' she whispered with a shy smile making me once again thank the gods that I'd met this amazing woman.

Well I be damned, if she were going to offer that type of statement then I'd be a fool not to take her up on it. 'As you wish,' I murmured. 'Suck me first then I'm going to screw you so hard that you scream my name. You are not allowed to come until I say you can,' I added as a little added extra challenge for her. With one more cheeky smile, Stella lowered her head.

My eyes rolled back in my head and the lids fluttered shut at the first flicks of her tongue on my throbbing shaft. *Fuck*, that felt amazing. I tried my best to let Stella do her own thing, but as she upped the pace and strength of her sucking I couldn't help but twist my fingers in her hair and thrust myself into her waiting mouth hoping I wouldn't go too deep and make her gag, but almost beyond the point where I cared. Fuck, I really was such a prick, I thought absently as pleasure began to build and swirl in my abdomen.

Cupping my balls with one hand Stella used her other hand on my thigh to steady herself as I thrust her face back and forth on my groin until I was almost forcing my length down her throat on each stroke. Jesus she was good at this. I could feel my orgasm fast approaching and tightened my grip in her hair, but as I did, Stella's rhythm faltered slightly and I felt her shudder against me. Thinking that perhaps I'd pushed her too far I looked down and met her gaze, but it was only when I saw her apologetic look, dilated pupils, and flushed cheeks that I realised she was shuddering not because she was gagging, but because she was climaxing.

Holy shit. For a second I was totally dumbfounded, Stella had actually climaxed merely from pleasuring me ... and not only pleasuring me, but letting me use her as I wanted ... and believe me when I say I was being far from gentle. Good God, this woman was truly amazing. Not allowing herself much time to recover, Stella took over where I had paused and finished me off with a few mind-numbingly hard sucks that had me growling like a wild animal and filling her mouth with my spurting climax as my hips jolted uncontrollably against her face.

As she released me with a soft popping sound, Stella looked up at me with wide, remorse-filled eyes. 'I'm so sorry, Sir ...' she murmured, chewing nervously on her lower lip.

'You came without permission,' I stated, still fucking amazed by the occurrence. For once, I allowed my eyes to burn into hers and saw her pupils were still dilated from her orgasm. Truth be told, I loved the fact that giving me pleasure clearly gave her just as much enjoyment, but I wouldn't let her know that just yet.

'I didn't mean to ... it was only a small one ...' she murmured, sounding genuinely mortified to have broken my rule.

I stared at her for several more seconds still amazed at how perfectly she was suited to being a submissive, after all the relationship was all based around wanting to ensure the other partners pleasure, which clearly she did. Finally, I couldn't take her miserable expression any longer and I allowed a small smile to curve the corner of my lips. 'Come here,' I murmured, dragging her to standing and slamming my lips onto hers in a kiss that probably expressed a bit more emotion that I really wanted it to.

'You're amazing, you know that?' I murmured as I scooped her up and strode back to the bed, but apparently, Stella didn't understand what I meant.

'You just climaxed with absolutely no stimulation, Stella ...' I began.

'I know ... I'm sorry, it's never happened before. I don't

know what happened ...' she muttered, almost sounding ashamed. She should never be ashamed of an orgasm, even if I had told her not to. Gripping her chin, I raised her wary face to mine, although kept my focus just below her eyes.

'Don't apologise. I think I understand ... pleasing me, does it turn you on that much? So much that you climaxed from it?' I asked, still unsure exactly *how* that could happen, but Stella's eyes flew open wide and she smiled a small, shy smile, nodding as she bit her lip. 'Yes. I like making you happy.'

I knew I was staring at her but I couldn't help it. She liked pleasing me? *Fuck*. Stella could have no idea just how much those words thrilled me, because I fucking loved her making me happy too.

NINETEEN – STELLA

It was five past six on the following Friday night and I'd literally only just arrived at Nathan's for my weekend stay when the door to my room unexpectedly swung open and Nathan strode in without so much as a knock. 'Put these on and meet me in the room opposite in five minutes,' he instructed cryptically, before depositing a plastic carrier bag on the chair and leaving.

I watched the door shut and raised my eyebrows, charming, there was no "Good evening, Stella" or "Have you had a nice week?" Just a snapped-out demand and a scowl. Admittedly, Nathan looked pretty good when he scowled, all dark and broody, but still, a little civility wouldn't go amiss.

I'd assumed he was still at work when I'd arrived five minutes ago because there'd been no sign of him in the apartment, but quite clearly he was here, and more obviously, he wasn't in the best of moods. Great, dour Nathan, just what I needed to get my weekend off to a shitty start.

Sighing at the ever-changing mood swings of my obsessive dominant my eyes moved back to the carrier bag and crinkled as I frowned. How odd, and I couldn't for the life of me remember what was in the room opposite … nope, I was blank, the apartment was so bloody large that I still kept confusing the layout. Peering inside the carrier bag I raised my eyebrows in surprise, either he had some weird ideas of kinky, or he had something totally non-sexual in mind for me.

After visiting the bathroom to freshen up I dutifully began to dress myself in the clothes I found in Nathan's bag, noticing that everything had been purchased in exactly my size. He'd either been snooping in my wardrobe or had a scarily accurate

123

eye for sizing up a ladies figure. No doubt from thoroughly assessing a string of different women in the past, I thought with a scowl – an image I didn't like in the slightest. Frowning I looked down at myself, now dressed in black shorts – rather short shorts, actually – a sports bra and a pale pink vest top. Donning the trainers that were also in the bag, I opened my door, padded across the hall and found myself walking into the small gym. Ah yes, that's right, I'd forgotten because although I've used the gym enough times I'd always accessed it from the other door off the main hallway and never through this door.

Nathan was already running at quite a speed on one of the two treadmills in the room as I entered and I took a second to admire his stunning physique. This was particularly easy seeing as he was only wearing running shorts and trainers and nothing else. Lovely, with just a hint of sweat glistening on his exposed neck and taut back to really make my mind race.

'You're late, I said five minutes,' he barked in way of a greeting completely ruining the lovely daydream I had been having of him and me getting downright sweaty together on the yoga mats in the corner of the room.

Rolling my eyes, I ignored his blunt words and glanced around the room. 'Fitness?' I questioned as I allowed my eyes to roam the room again, hoping to see some other sex-related reason for being in here. Weights machines, treadmills, stretching mats, it was very well fitted, and all disappointingly non-sexual. 'On a Friday night?' As far as I was concerned, Friday nights were either for wine and takeaways, or wine and Nathan, not slogging my guts out on a treadmill.

'Yes. A healthy lifestyle is very important,' Nathan stated, watching me in the mirror as he continued to run, his body working fluidly with the machine, chest muscles rippling, and posture perfect. Christ, he really was a beautiful specimen of masculinity.

'I think you keep me fit enough,' I joked dryly, eyeing the treadmill warily, running was something I *did not* do; far too many opportunities for falling over and making a fool of myself. On the occasions I'd used Nathan's gym I'd rowed, or done some yoga or Pilates on the matted area, *never* running.

'Come, get on,' he instructed, indicating to the other treadmill with a brief wave of his hand before his arms went back to the job of pumping by his sides and powering him along.

'Running?' I questioned out loud like a complete imbecile. 'No, I don't really run, actually I prefer the cross trainer but seeing as you don't have one ...' But my comment dried in my throat as Nathan slammed his fist down on the emergency stop button of his running machine, making me jump and let out a small yelp. Cruising off the slowing roller, he was standing opposite me before I'd even seen him move, his face glistening with sweat as he glowered across at me giving me his signal by raising his eyebrows and pointing to a spot just to the left of him.

Shit, shit, and double shit. Nathan hardly ever demanded I move next to him to submit. Obviously, he was *really* mad. Glancing at his livid expression, I corrected my first thoughts. He wasn't just mad, Nathan was utterly furious – surely this temper wasn't all because I was a few minutes late?

In that moment I immediately regretted my stupid cockiness, then stumbling towards him I did my best to don my submissive exterior; quickly averting my eyes, linking my fingers in front of myself, and then when I reached his side I made the split second decision to also drop to my knees. I remembered that Nathan had once told me that kneeling was one of the most submissive postures and I was desperately hoping that this gesture might lighten his mood.

Internally I was kicking myself for being so relaxed with him in the first place, but sometimes on a Friday night after a week at work it took me a while to switch between my lifestyles, tonight being one of those nights, but with Nathan looking like he was ready to punish me on the spot I was certainly getting a brisk reminder of where I was right now.

'I'm sorry, Sir,' I mumbled. Fuck, he could actually be terrifying at times, this moment now being a prime example of one of those times. I could see his beautiful chest rapidly rising and falling under his heavy breathing and I briefly wondered if it was due to his exertion on the running machine or his anger towards me. I could just about see him chewing on the inside of his lip, seemingly a sign of tension for Nathan, as he stared at me through narrowed eyes, assessing my kneeling position. But from my low level on the floor, I couldn't make out what his verdict was.

'As fuckable as you look kneeling down there Stella, that won't help you now,' Nathan ground out and I felt the hairs on my neck rise at his ominous tone. Reaching down he gripped my shoulders and tugged me none too gently to a standing position. 'Running,' he stated again in a deadly tone. 'For 20 minutes, yes?' Standing back Nathan then crossed his arms and watched me to see what I would do, he seemed to be almost challenging me to defy him, but with the look of barely leashed fury burning in his eyes there was no way I was holding out on him again.

Not wanting to push my luck I quickly nodded my acceptance and began to move towards the treadmill.

'Did you just *nod* at me?' Nathan demanded, his tone so low and gritty that I barely heard it. Bugger, I *had* nodded, and he'd warned me before that if I ever did it again he'd punish me … would he punish me now? Would I enjoy it more than a run? Quite possibly, because I bloody hated running.

Seeing as Nathan didn't seem in the mood to find out, I mumbled an apology. 'Sorry, Sir …' I ducked my head as I passed him and climbed onto the treadmill. Pressing the quick start button, I started with a fast walk before catching sight of Nathan's glare in the mirror. *Jeez*, this man was such a control freak, so with a sigh I increased the speed to a run and began plodding along unhappily. Giving a jerky nod of satisfaction Nathan finally climbed back on his running machine alongside mine and continued his workout without saying another word.

After exactly 20 minutes, Nathan slowed his runner to a walk and leant over doing the same thing to mine. I was breathing hard by now, but as I walked to cool down, I felt quite proud of myself for completing the run without stopping or falling off. Actually, I'd quite enjoyed it, perhaps adding a run to my usual weekly fitness wouldn't be such a bad experience after all. A good bit of music would have made it more bearable though, perhaps I'd look into getting some little speakers for my iPod.

With a pleased huff, I stepped from the treadmill and wandered over to the corner to grab a towel to wipe my sweaty face. Turning back I paused by a large contraption that was complete with weights and a pull up bar. I had no idea what the other bits did, something for the arms and legs presumably. Smiling at how bad I was at chin-ups I turned to say as much to Nathan only to find him standing watching me intently from under furrowed brows with his jaw clenched tightly and his arms folded across his chest.

I swallowed loudly and my heart rate accelerated even faster in my chest. He looked scarily formidable, but enticingly sexy all at once. Instinctively I went to twirl my thumb ring, but I'd taken it off before the run and found my nail digging into my bare skin instead. Nathan was obviously still angry with me. Very angry if the tight white skin on either side of his taught mouth was anything to go by. *Bugger*, I'd hoped the run might have cleared his anger, but apparently not. Licking my dry lips, I hesitantly made my way towards him and handed him a spare towel before linking my hands and averting my eyes.

'I'm sorry for my behaviour earlier, Sir,' I said softly. 'I wasn't thinking.'

'It's a little late for that, Stella, and I believe I warned you what would happen if you were ever rude enough to nod at me again,' Nathan muttered as he used the towel to dry off his chest before rubbing it vigorously through his hair to soak up the sweat leaving it a mused and spiky mess flopping onto his face. Damn, he hadn't forgotten about my nod, would he punish me? Here in the gym? My heart rate rocketed even higher as I wondered what he'd do to me.

Chucking the towel aside I watched as Nathan used his foot to push a low fitness step towards me until it nudged against my feet. 'Stand on this.'

Frowning, I did as I was told and stepped up even though I had no idea what he was going to make me do next. Muscle training for my legs perhaps? After running almost flat out for 20 minutes, I seriously doubted if my legs could cope with any more training tonight. Surely, a run was enough?

'Raise your arms and hold the bar,' Nathan instructed, indicating to the chin up bar, but I hesitated, I'd heard that dark tone of voice before from Nathan, he wasn't thinking about exercise now, he was planning something kinky. The idea instantly sent a jolt of lust thumping to my groin, but with his foul mood I was still wavering on whether this was a good idea right now.

'But I'm all sweaty,' I protested weakly knowing that a bit of bodily fluid wouldn't stop Nathan if he had his mind set on something. What can I say? One thing I've learnt in my weeks with Nathan is that even with his obsessive hygiene he's very tenacious when it comes to his pursuit of kink.

'Do it,' Nathan snapped. And my heartbeat fluttered so violently in my chest I wondered if it was going to crunch to a standstill. His tone left no doubt of his anger and there really was no other way I could think to delay him, so I reluctantly raised my arms and took hold of the cool metal pull up bar. This was hardly my best ever pose and yet still I was getting horny. Wincing I glanced down and saw the dark sweat marks on my vest top. Gross, although seeing Nathan sweating didn't bother me in the slightest so maybe the feeling was mutual.

Bending down Nathan began to sort through a box of sports equipment apparently looking for something in particular. Boxing gloves were discarded to the side, as were small dumbbells and a stopwatch, before he grunted in acknowledgement, picked up a skipping rope and, without another word, proceeded to tie my wrists to the bar. Bloody hell! This was certainly new, but even with his appalling mood I couldn't help but feel aroused by it, it was just something about Nathan and his commanding air that got me hot every frigging time I was near him.

'Hold on, otherwise this will rub your skin,' he instructed and I immediately did as I was told.

Once I was trussed up like some Victorian wench and unable to escape Nathan bent and removed my trainers and socks one by one, before coming to stand behind me and looking over my shoulder so I could see us both reflected in the large wall length mirrors than lined the gym. Nathan's gaze was lowered from mine but there was no hiding the dark intent hidden behind his beautiful lashes. Wow, the view of us like this – Nathan commanding, cool, and deliciously shirtless – and me tied up completely at his mercy, was so frigging hot I felt like I was melting on the spot.

Moving away from me, Nathan began to slowly circle me like a predator checking out his latest prey. He was clearly trying to build up the anticipation, but he really needn't have bothered, I was quivering, wet, and way past ready. Jeez, the way my heart was thumping I wondered why I'd bothered with the run, this was obviously just as good for my cardio as any treadmill time.

'I'm going to spank you for your earlier disobedience.' *What!* Now that I had not expected! I'd thought his punishment might be no orgasm for me – or no sex full stop – but actual spanking? My breath caught in my throat as I processed his words ... He was going to punish me while I was tied to a weights machine ... was this guy for real?

To be honest I couldn't quite believe it, but sure enough a second later he reached round me and begun his fun. First off Nathan merely flattened his hands on my quivering belly before splaying his fingers out and massaging me as he slowly began to slide his hands down inside my shorts and underwear, pushing them down my legs until they slipped to my ankles.

His next move was the most unexpected though, when he kicked the frigging step out from underneath my feet! Fuck! I was jerked into mid-air and left clutching at the bar above me with my feet kicking and swinging in surprise. It was all very inelegant really, my shorts and knickers fell to the floor as I desperately flailed around like a wriggling eel trying to support my own weight.

Eventually I worked out that if I stopped wriggling it was far easier to hold on, although thankfully the way Nathan had tied the rope did at least give my wrists some support.

'You will receive eight in total. Two for making me wait. I detest lateness, Stella, you know this and yet you still push me. If I say come to me in five minutes, I mean five fucking minutes,' he growled. Blimey, he really had his knickers in a twist today, and I wondered what the hell had happened to make him so grouchy. Perhaps it was still the work issues he'd mentioned last weekend.

My mind was brought back from its wanderings when with no further warning Nathan stepped back and landed a hard slap on my left buttock before repeating the treatment to my right one. The impact from his contact made me yelp softly as my body swayed forwards and backwards like a giant, half-naked, human pendulum. As weird as it was I couldn't help but watch everything in the mirror and to be honest the bizarre scene unravelling in front of me was really rather arousing. This was so peculiar, but somehow such a turn on at the same time.

Leaning in close to my ear Nathan briefly grazed his teeth along my neck in my favourite sensitive spot making me mewl softly and try to press into the contact. 'These next two are for your insolence. It's not an attractive quality Stella, and you *will not* nod at me again.' My lips pressed together to hold in the remarks that flew to my brain as Nathan once again stepped back and spanked me twice, harder this time, before caressing my behind with both his hands. I couldn't help let out a muted cry, but it was more from the shock of my strange hanging position than any severe pain really.

'These last four are because you questioned me. Never question me Stella,' he told me in a tone so dark but delicious that a shudder ran through my entire body. 'I always have your best interests in mind so if I ask you to do something, you do it. Understand?'

By this point Nathan's head was close to my neck again, his breath hot on my skin and I realised I was panting wantonly and leaning into him like a desperate strumpet. 'Yes Sir,' I breathed between gasps as Nathan landed the final four slaps on my tingling behind with increasing force. Each spank made the throbbing at the apex of my thighs ten times worse, or better, whichever way you want to think of it, but then Nathan's final two contacts were lower than before and sent such a rush of desire shooting between my legs that I very nearly came.

How peculiar that even in this strange half-hanging, half

bound position I could be so turned on that I was practically dripping.

Moving in front of me Nathan slowly removed his trainers, running shorts, and boxers until he was stood before me in all his naked splendidness. My eyes widened as I took him in. Apparently, it was possible to be absolutely livid while also fully aroused. Christ he was so lean and lithe that it never failed to distract me from all other thoughts.

After giving me a second to absorb his stunning maleness, Nathan dropped to his knees and then gripped my thighs painfully hard before he suddenly lowered his face with a dark, lusty look flickering in his eyes. Parting my legs as wide as they would go, he dipped forwards and immediately ran a wet swipe of his tongue up the entire length of my folds, making my legs tense with pleasure and instantly pushing away my lingering concern over the fact that I was still sweaty from my run.

'You are not allowed to come,' he stated from his position in between my legs. So that was to be my next punishment, but his hot breath on my skin was doing nothing to cool my desire and not helping in holding me back from the forbidden climax one little bit.

What he was doing to me was exquisite, but over the next minute or so the pressure on my wrists began to get too much. I'd never been particularly strong in my arms and it was getting too much for me as gradually I felt my grip faltering finger by finger, with the rope taking more and more of my weight until it was painfully cutting into my skin.

I hadn't meant to, but a soft moan escaped my lips. It must have indicated more pain than pleasure because Nathan looked up at me questioningly. As ridiculous as it was I didn't want him to stop, even with the burning pain in my wrists, but reluctantly I confessed. 'My wrists ...I can't hold on any longer, it hurts, Sir,' I explained breathlessly.

Looping his hands under my dangling legs Nathan flicked my knees over his shoulders and raised his body slightly so that I was effectively sitting on his shoulders with my lady bits plastered up against his face. I couldn't help a smile slipping to my lips, but as provocative as the position was it also eased the pressure on my wrists. 'Better?' he enquired. 'Or shall I stop?'

There was no way in hell I was going to ask him to stop. 'That's better Sir, thank you,' I confirmed breathlessly. 'Please don't stop.' Looking down I blushed, Nathan literally had his face buried between my legs. My sweaty, quivery legs. But my embarrassment was soon forgotten as Nathan took up his teasing again using his tongue and teeth to lick and nip at me until I squeezed my thighs around his head in an attempt at holding back the climax that was now threatening to wash over me. I mustn't come, not until he gave me permission, and although I'd never actively defied one of his commands I knew without a doubt that with his bad mood today Nathan would definitely punish me if I did.

While the delicious sensations of a near orgasm clenched my insides, Nathan suddenly stood up. In one swift movement, he shifted me from his shoulders into a tight grip around my hips where he wasted no time thrusting himself inside me and groaning so deeply it sounded like a growl next to my ear. Wow, talk about a speedy manoeuvre, I wasn't even sure how he'd managed that. 'Wrap your legs around me,' he ordered gruffly, but I was ahead of him on that, already linking my ankles behind his back as he reached up and undid the rope around my wrists.

Once my arms were free I slipped them around Nathan's neck, greedily digging them into the strong muscle of his shoulders for support as he turned us sideways and slammed my back against the mirrored wall causing the whole thing to rattle. Burying his head in the crook of my neck Nathan held me firmly by the hips so I was pinned to the wall, and then began to grind against me, sending curling waves of pleasure spiralling through me.

Oh God, this was heavenly. When Nathan started a faster rhythm that was hitting just the right spot inside me I found myself biting my own lip hard with the effort not to come. Trying to distract myself from my imminent orgasm, I briefly considered his mood again. I knew he was still mad at me, because he was plunging himself inside me almost violently, that plus the fact that he hadn't kissed me at all indicated to me his lingering annoyance. I had quickly learnt in the early stages of our relationship that we never kissed if he was in a bad mood; it seemed to be his way of denying me something he knew I enjoyed. Mind you, I was enjoying myself quite a lot right now too.

'Come,' Nathan suddenly demanded through gritted teeth and I immediately opened the floodgates on my muscles relaxing my almost painfully contracted groin allowing an orgasm like no other to rip through my body like a tidal wave. 'Fuck!' As I spasmed around his body, Nathan tensed and also found his release, before finally stilling and resting his head on my shoulder breathing raggedly. We stayed like that for several minutes, not that I could have gone anywhere because I was trapped against the wall and wrapped around him like a limpet, both of us breathing hard and trying to recover ourselves before Nathan finally leant back and eased himself out of me.

I winced at the empty, slightly sore feeling between my legs as I watched Nathan pulling on his running shorts and picking up a large roll of tissue before turning to me. 'Clean up the mess,' he instructed bluntly, as he indicated to the drips of sweat and other bodily fluids that surrounded the area where we had just had sex.

Charming. Clearly even sex hadn't lightened his mood.

Briefly rubbing my wrists I wordlessly took the tissue and after putting my knickers back on to restore a little of my dignity I bent to wipe the floor. After watching me with narrowed eyes Nathan then left the room and I sighed heavily once again feeling rather overwhelmed by the experiences my dominant bad boy was giving me.

Nathan was like a force of nature; once you pissed him off you needed to get the hell out of the area or batten down the hatches and ride out the storm. A grin stretched my mouth, it wasn't like I particularly minded riding out Nathan's storms – he was certainly never dull, that was for sure – but I did feel slightly guilty for getting him so annoyed in the first place. A small shrug raised my shoulders. Oh well, I probably wouldn't see him again tonight and no doubt he'd be over it by the time we met for breakfast in the morning.

My head popped up less than a minute later when Nathan came striding back in taking me completely by surprise. With his strop, I'd thought that he'd retire for the night and be done with me, but apparently not.

'Leave that, come and sit here,' he ordered impatiently causing me to widen my eyes in surprise. I couldn't quite put my finger on it but he sounded a little odd. Doing as I was asked I dumped the tissue down on the floor and made my way across to him cautiously. He indicated to a chair with a jerk of his thumb and I lowered myself down next to him where he proceeded to examine my wrists intently with a frown. Glancing down at them again, I saw that although they weren't really that sore they were actually quite red from where the rope had chafed me. Ah, so this was what was bothering him.

Producing a medical ice pack from his pocket Nathan carefully wrapped it around my wrists as I sat silently, letting him do his thing and tend to me how he wished. It really was a bit too cold on my already sore skin, not that I'd mention that, but then as if reading my mind Nathan removed the ice, wrapped it in a T-shirt – probably the one he'd striped off before running – and then nodded. 'Keep this on for ten minutes,' he muttered, before walking over and bending to finish cleaning the floor.

Wow. This was quite a turnabout for the books. I was shocked, first his apparent concern for me, and now cleaning up so I wouldn't have to do it later. A small affectionate smile twitched on my lips as I watched him work, his frown line remaining in place the entire time. Who are you and what have you done with my inconsiderate dominant?

Depositing the tissues in the bin Nathan walked towards me and opened the door that led to the bedroom corridor. 'Come, you'll be more comfortable resting in your room.'

Once I was sat comfortably on my bed, Nathan fussed about me checking the ice packs repeatedly to check that they were still wrapped firmly around my wrists and then with a tight nod he left the room without saying a single word. The man was such an enigma. Huffing out a lengthy breath, I shook my head at his neurotic ways, I mean who ties someone up and spanks them only to panic about some small bruising afterwards? It was like he was a complete walking contradiction.

Musing over Nathan and his peculiarities, I sank back into the pillows, closed my eyes and let the coolness of the icepack relax me for a few minutes.

I must have dropped off to sleep because a knock on my door woke me and after glancing at the clock to see that quarter of an hour had passed I blearily looked over to see Nathan peering around the door. He seemed to be bearing gifts again as he had a tube of something in his hands, but I was more distracted by his freshly showered appearance, his blond hair still wet and brushed back from his face and his heavenly scent hitting my nostrils, reminding me of just how much I loved his shower gel – or perhaps it was his aftershave, I didn't know. Freshly showered Nathan in all his spicy musky glory was my favourite scent on the planet.

'You kept them on,' he said with an approving nod at the ice packs. Removing them Nathan frowned again and gently poked at my wrists. 'It wasn't meant to bruise,' he muttered in a low tone that I suspected was as much of an apology as I was going to get.

'I don't think it will bruise, my skin's just pink from the cold ice,' I murmured, trying to placate him. They really didn't hurt at all.

'I have some arnica cream here; you can leave it on overnight. Grab a shower and I'll put it on for you,' Nathan said holding up the tube.

'Just leave it on the side. I'll be fine, honestly.' But the forceful look on Nathan's face made me sigh with resignation and push myself from the bed in the direction of the en-suite. Sometimes it was just easier to give in than fight him.

Soaping myself up and washing felt strange knowing that Nathan was sat just next door so I had a pretty speedy shower, wrapped myself firmly in my towel and then emerged into the bedroom. I paused awkwardly as I stood in my bedroom still just wrapped in a towel with Nathan watching me intently from the bed. All my clothes were in the drawers across the other side of the room, should I select what I wanted and go back to the bathroom to dress? It seemed a bit of a waste of time, but with Nathan watching me like a hawk I suddenly felt hugely self-conscious.

Flicking my gaze back to the bed I saw Nathan suppressing a smile at my dilemma, *bastard*, but then he flashed me his custom dark and dangerous look instead. 'I've seen you naked so many times now, Stella, surely you're not embarrassed?'

His words were like a challenge to me, well fine, two could play at that game. Turning to my dressing table, I kept the towel firmly wrapped around myself as I vigorously brushed my hair and planned what to do, then with my idea set I walked across the room towards my chest of drawers and casually let the towel slip from my body and pool on the floor. I couldn't see Nathan's face, but I gained a lot of satisfaction from the gasp I heard from him as I stepped into a particularly sexy pair of black lace French knickers. As stupid as it was I loved the fact that he seemed to be just as affected by me as I constantly was by him.

Reaching back into the drawer I dug around for a minute until I found the matching bra and then took my time to wiggle my hips as I made a show of sliding my arms into the bra and reaching behind myself to fasten it.

My little tease had got me so preoccupied that I hadn't heard Nathan move, but suddenly his arms were wrapping around me from behind and pulling me firmly against him trapping my arms, and half-done bra, at my sides. 'Fuck, Stella, the things you do to me.' he hissed, burying his head in my neck as his hands explored the fine silk of my lingerie. Likewise, buddy, I thought, as my eyes rolled closed on a moan.

Turning me in his arms, Nathan sought my mouth with a desperate kiss and ravished me with such an intensity that I was soon clinging to his biceps for stability as my body hummed with a new arousal. To my complete frustration Nathan ripped his lips from mine just as we were getting to the good part, and then stood back gently taking my wrists in his hands and examining the light pink marks that were still visible.

'Let me put this cream on before I lose control and forget all about it,' he muttered, guiding me to the bed and undoing the tube. Was he seriously going to leave me turned on like this without relief? Damn him and his stupidly good self-control!

With exceptionally delicate fingers Nathan set about gently rubbing the arnica cream on both of my wrists before finally placing my hands down and resealing the tube. I watched his posture with interest; he was more slumped than usual, and to me it looked a lot like Nathan was still feeling guilty about marking me, so I gently reached out and stroked his forearm. 'It's not your fault … Sir.' I'd become a bit lazy with using his title lately, but added it hoping it might relax him. 'I wasn't thinking when I first went into the gym tonight and I upset you, I'm sorry, I hadn't switched off from work I guess, I wound you up, so if anything it's my fault, not yours.'

Grunting his acknowledgement of my words Nathan suddenly stood up and began pacing the room repeatedly as he chewed furiously on the inside of his lower lip, apparently still beating himself up about my wrists. Stopping just as suddenly as he had started Nathan looked at me as his expression cleared briefly, then reaching into his pocket he removed a long thin box. 'I nearly forgot … I got you this,' he said as he handed me the box.

I stared at the box in my hand as if it had just sprouted four heads, a gift? For me? *From Nathan?* Well, that was certainly a nice surprise. 'Open it,' he prompted me, so I did, immediately drawing in a sharp breath at the contents. Crikey, laid on a deep blue velvet cushion was a necklace made up of three rows of diamonds and decorated with three small flowers made up of light blue gems. It was absolutely beautiful.

'It's a new collar – well, a choker, really – but this one is less obvious so you can wear it when you are out if you want to. It would please me greatly if you always wore it,' Nathan murmured. Another collar … Was this his way of claiming me? He'd said that he would replace my simple training one if and when he thought our relationship was developing. There was no way of getting away from the fact that we were dynamite in bed together so perhaps he was now viewing me as a more permanent fixture. Deciding not to ruin the moment with my stupid naïve questions I stayed silent and instead examined the necklace more carefully. Letting out a soft gasp, I ran my fingers along the stones, in awe of its simple beauty.

'Do you like it?' Nathan enquired in an odd voice.

'Yes, I love it.' I raised my eyes to his before remembering to avert my gaze. 'Will you put it on me, please Sir?'

Lowering himself to the bed again Nathan sat behind me and removed the thin leather collar before replacing it with his purchase. It felt heavier, like it had more of a claim over me, and I hadn't been kidding when I said I loved it. 'When you wear it, it should remind you that you are mine,' he said as his fingers brushed against my skin teasingly. 'You belong to me,' he murmured.

As a 20-something, independent businesswoman I should have hated the way Nathan was laying claim to me, but I simply didn't. I wanted to be his, and although I knew he wouldn't say it out loud, this new token of our relationship proved that in some way, Nathan was mine too.

'Thank you,' I gushed, my hand coming up to stroke the chain again, knowing that I would never take it off. Looking up at the confusingly neurotic man who had become such a major part of my life of late, I saw him frowning at my over the top gratitude, so sighing I cleared my expression, settled myself back in the pillows, shook my head in disbelief at all that had happened in the last hour and a half and then rolled my eyes as Nathan wordlessly left my room.

Crazy. Punished, then given a present. What a start to the weekend!

TWENTY – STELLA

Several weeks had now passed since the official start to my arrangement with Nathan – for some reason my dirty little mind judged 'the start' as the time we started sleeping together, not when we'd first met – and I had to say things were going surprisingly well. Nathan demanded a large percentage of my time while I was at his place over the weekends, not that I was complaining, but inevitably, at some point he would have work to do. I used these times as an opportunity to catch up on some work myself, use the gym in his apartment for some yoga, or do a little reading.

Work today had been deadly slow, ugh, I had been desperate to leave all day, so in the end I'd clocked out spot on five and headed straight to Nathan's in the hope that he'd be home early too and might fancy brightening up my day with a nice start to the weekend. Unfortunately he hadn't been home and I now found myself in the gym on the treadmill – yes, me on a treadmill – racking up my fifth kilometre of the evening and feeling rather proud of myself. The sound of the front door slamming followed by pacing footsteps disturbed my thoughts.

'Stella! Stella? Where the fuck are you?' Nathan's yelling voice easily travelled through the walls into the gym and I winced at his apparent distress. Was something wrong? I could hear him thumping and banging his way around the apartment apparently searching for me. Rolling my eyes, I slowed the treadmill. Nathan was home then. Jeez, he sounded crazy, I hadn't even seen him tonight, what the hell could I have done wrong already?

Slamming my hand down on the stop button of the treadmill, I jumped off and then after wrapping a towel around my sweaty neck I immediately went in the direction of his voice – the gym door that led to the bedroom corridor.

Opening the door I stepped out in time to see him striding around my bedroom looking frantic before he caught sight of me in the corridor and immediately paced out and joined me.

'Stella. You're here,' he said on a rushed breath. I raised my eyebrows at the relief I detected in not only his tone, but his facial expression too, then noticed that he was still holding his car keys in one hand and briefcase in the other as if he had come searching for me straight away. How odd, had he thought I wasn't going to show tonight? Had that worried him? Once again, I was left baffled by this thoroughly confusing man.

'I was running,' I said needlessly, given my gym clothing and sweat covered face it was probably fairly obvious what I had been doing. In front of my eyes, I watched as Nathan seemed to get a grip of himself and return to the normal cool and calm character that I was used to. That had been a very peculiar episode.

'Running?' he scoffed with a half-smile. 'How ironic,' he added on a murmur and I couldn't help suppress my own smile too. After the fuss I had made last week, the irony of this situation was not lost on me either, but strangely last week's wrangle with the treadmill had actually been quite enjoyable and I had been looking forward to another run all week. *Looking forward to a run*. Wow, they would never have been words in my vocabulary if I hadn't met Nathaniel Jackson.

'Finish your workout if you like, but I thought that for a change perhaps we'd go out tonight,' Nathan said, pocketing his keys and loosening his tie, a movement I found rather distracting as small amounts of his skin became uncovered tempting me to lean in and taste it.

Dragging my eyes away from temptation my mind stuck on his final words … go out? So far, all of our encounters had been based at his place; we never went for meals or did anything that could be misconstrued as 'romantic', so it would be fair to say I was rather stunned at Nathan's announcement that he was taking me out tonight.

I had no chance to enquire where we might be going though

because he finally pulled his tie free and turned on the spot. 'We'll leave in an hour. Wear something fancy, clothes appropriate for a bar,' he instructed me briskly before abruptly heading to his bedroom and slamming the door. I chewed nervously on my lower lip. Going out with Nathan? My dominant? *In public?* I made a low, apprehensive humming noise in the back of my throat as I considered this turn of events. One thing was sure though, from his demeanour it certainly didn't seem like tonight was going to be a romantic occasion.

I had a nervous expression on my face as I applied my make-up, but I'd done as Nathan asked – I was wearing something 'fancy'. My favourite little black dress with some killer heels and the choker necklace he gave me to wear in lieu of a collar. It was also about the only smart outfit in my limited wardrobe here. My hand was shaking so much that I had trouble with my mascara and for several minutes I seriously thought that I'd either be going out with none on, or alternatively have it smeared and dabbed all over my face.

Finally I was happy with my appearance; my hair was loose and behaving rather nicely, my outfit looked good, and I managed to wrestle my nerves under control for long enough to finish my make-up without looking like Alice Cooper.

OK, let's do this. I walked back out to the living room with eleven minutes of my hour left but the sight before me made me suddenly forget how to breathe. Nathan looked *stunning*. The thing with Nathan is he always looks good. Casual jeans and a T-shirt? Looks good. Three-piece work suit? Looks good. Sweaty gym gear? Looks good. But bloody hell, does he carry off the smart casual thing well. He was wearing a black, long-sleeved shirt and grey trousers that clung oh-so nicely to his thighs ... I suspected there was a jacket around here somewhere too, which would no doubt emphasise his gloriously broad shoulders. I wanted to swear out loud at just how explicitly edible he looked, but I knew he wouldn't like me cursing so I did it in my head instead – fuck me, this man was fucking sex on legs.

Obviously hearing my approach Nathan turned to inspect

me. I say 'inspect' and not 'admire', because that's exactly what it felt like, an examination, his face remained impassive but his eyes swept from the tips of my toes right to the top of my head as he decided if I was suitable or not. Had I passed muster? I had no idea, and he wouldn't make eye contact with me so I really couldn't tell.

Picking up a jacket that matched his trousers Nathan stalked towards me and paused just by my side. 'Very fucking sexy, Stella,' he murmured, still not looking at me, before lightly running his fingers around the choker with an appreciative grunt and then heading to the front door leaving me flushed and wobbling in his wake like the pathetic woman I was. Smiling, I followed him. He liked my outfit and that made me feel ridiculously pleased with myself.

As we descended in the lift, my nerves kicked back into gear. We'd never been out in public together; would this be like a date? I really had no idea. I must have been chomping on my bottom lip at a fair rate of knots because Nathan reached up wordlessly and used his thumb to halt my chewing. 'I can see you're nervous, Stella, don't be.' It wasn't exactly a great pep talk, was it? But at least he'd acknowledged that this was out of my comfort zone, I suppose.

'How do I act? Do I call you Sir?' Did I want to call him Sir if we were out together? I usually only used the title in the bedroom, but I really had no idea how to approach this. God, I wished we had just stayed in and had a nice, normal shag now. Not that sex with Nathan was ever what I would call 'normal', but still.

'I tell you what, as you're nervous and still relatively new to this we'll go to Club Twist. Everyone there is like-minded so that should ease your nerves.' OK, that sounded a little better, although thinking back to some of the stuff that was being done last time – eye-popping displays of sexuality – I wasn't sure it would particularly ease my nerves.

Apparently, still in thought Nathan suddenly narrowed his eyes and briefly looked down at me. 'With regards to calling me Sir, I'll leave it up to you, Stella, but just know that it would please me greatly if you did so.' Right, no pressure there, then. I either call him Sir and make him happy or don't call him Sir and piss him off. I rolled my eyes – over the past few weeks I'd learnt that happy Nathan equalled smoking-hot sex sessions, whereas pissed off Nathan usually lead to a rather quicker and less satisfying outcome for me, but enjoyable sex for him. I knew which option I wanted tonight – smoking hot – and I scoffed at my mind's dirty path. Ah well, it was only a word, wasn't it? I'm sure I could manage it for one night.

When we arrived at Club Twist, Nathan used a different entrance to the front one on the main road, choosing instead to park at the back and use a smaller private entrance. Walking in to the club again after so many weeks felt decidedly odd, especially as my mind was screaming 'it's a sex club!' at me repeatedly, but I did my best to look casual and unaffected as I prepared myself to look around the venue again.

I could do this; it wasn't like I was a prude or anything, so the sight of other people having sex shouldn't be an issue for me really … but then I promptly changed my mind as my eyes wandered to a dark corner behind the stage … *Oh, good God*, whatever was going on over there involved whips and belts and lots of red raw flesh being pounded rather ruthlessly by a multitude of men … *crikey*. As I gulped in a breath, my eyes widened significantly, and I swallowed rather loudly while reaching out and linking my trembling hand through Nathan's elbow for support.

'We can avoid that side of the bar,' Nathan murmured by my ear causing me to swing my head to find him watching the direct line of my gaze with a dark smile tweaking his mouth. 'I never thought you were into that type of stuff anyway,' he mused as his hooded gaze dropped curiously to where my hand was linked in his arm and clinging on for dear life.

Bugger, perhaps intimate contact like that was a no-no for Nathan, I had no idea, but as I went to pull my hand free he placed his on top and stilled me. 'No, leave it there,' he murmured. Wow, sometimes he really was surprisingly nice and, well … considerate.

Looking around the rest of the club, I was relieved to see it looked far more normal; people were dancing on the stage, drinking by the bar, and generally having a good time. Admittedly, there were several pedestals raised up with naked couples dancing on them and these were a little more racy, but still nothing to make me feel unduly uncomfortable.

'All the good stuff happens at a second stage behind this dance floor,' Nathan confided, pointing to another area round to the right. All the good stuff? What the hell did that mean? 'I'll show you later.' Oh God, well it looked like I'd been finding out fairly soon.

'So, what would you like to do, Stella?' I choked on thin air at his question and when I turned to him my eyes must have been as wide as saucers, did he expect me to join in? Have sex in front of all these people? Not a frigging chance!

'I was referring to whether you would like to dance or just get a drink, but I see from your expression that you misread me,' Nathan explained, obviously trying to withhold a smirk. Git.

'Sorry, Sir, I'm a little nervous,' I murmured softly. Nathan's face turned to mine as he heard my use of Sir and as well as feeling him tighten his arm around my hand I'm fairly sure I saw his arrogantly amused face soften, just slightly.

'I can see that, I keep forgetting you're new to all this. Perhaps no dancing just yet then,' he concluded. Dancing and me didn't really go well together at the best of times – I had serious co-ordination issues – let alone when my legs were rubbery and useless from nerves.

'No, maybe we could just watch a while?' I suggested, knowing full well that there was no way my wobbly legs would manage to carry me through any dancing without me looking like a complete prat.

This time Nathan couldn't conceal his amusement, and grinned broadly at me. 'I didn't realise you were a voyeur, Stella.'

What? My cheeks heated immediately, that was not what I meant and he must bloody well know it. 'I'm not … I just …' Huffing out a breath, I didn't bother to try and finish my sentence – he was clearly teasing me and it was working a treat. The thing was, though, even though I'd never watched anything like this before I was actually finding it all rather arousing. Or maybe that's just because I was here with Nathan and finding *him* arousing, which was really nothing new, I always felt in a constant state of arousal when I was near him, something I hoped never changed.

'I'll get us some drinks to help relax you,' Nathan suddenly commented before gently detaching my arm from his elbow and disappearing into the crowd, leaving me stood at the corner of the dance floor feeling like a lemon.

I'm quite a fan of people-watching normally, but stood here in Club Twist I was finding it rather difficult to know where to look. To my left was *that* corner with the whipping thing still taking place so I wasn't going to look there, to my right was a pedestal containing two naked women who were dancing and occasionally making out which made me feel a bit uncomfortable too, but if I just let my eyes wander the dance floor I inadvertently ended up rudely staring at some of the outfits being worn by a few of the dancers. Who knew that PVC was so popular? Surely, it would be horrifically sweaty to dance in? Or perhaps that was the point. Ugh.

Thankfully, Nathan returned with our drinks surprisingly quickly and led me silently around the side of the dance floor to a discreet alcove along the back wall. I noticed there were lots of them actually, all just big enough for a small round table and two chairs. The alcove was lit by a single candle and there was also a light gauze curtain across the entrance giving a hint of privacy, but still allowing you to watch the goings on in the bar, all in all it was quite cosy actually.

'We call these the watcher holes,' Nathan informed me, which seemed like an appropriate name to me. 'They offer a perfect view of both stages so you can sit and enjoy the shows in relative privacy.' Looking at me with a small smile, Nathan continued. 'Seeing as you expressed an interest in observing I thought it appropriate we sit here,' he added, obviously teasing me again. I quite liked this light-hearted version of Nathan that I was glimpsing tonight, but I couldn't help but think he wouldn't like it if I turned the tables and teased him back.

'I didn't mean I like to watch … it's not something I've ever done before,' I replied huffily, but then I paused as I realised my little lie. I might not have done this before, but now I was here I was quickly learning that actually, I did quite like to watch, only when Nathan was beside me though, I'd never dream of coming here on my own, not in a million years.

He must be a bloody mind reader because the next words from Nathan's mouth completely matched my own thoughts. 'But you like it and that fact embarrasses you?'

'No!' I lied instinctively, I was a terrible liar, but hopefully Nathan hadn't picked this up about me yet. Somehow it just felt wrong to admit it to him, did it make me a bit of a pervert if I was getting aroused watching this stuff?

One of Nathan's hands closed around my wrist and tugged sharply to get my attention. 'Stella, you are with *me*, if I ask you a question you do not lie to me, do you understand?' he spat in a fierce whisper. The sudden severity in his voice made me glance at him and bite down on my lip, gone was Mr Light-Hearted, now he was just plain angry with me. Damn it, how did he manage to read me so well?

'Yes, Sir, I understand,' I murmured softly trying to appease him.

'Are you enjoying the show?' he asked again, his tone still clipped.

My swallow was loud and uncomfortable in my throat. If the music hadn't been so loud around us I was fairly sure that Nathan would have heard it too. 'I feel like I shouldn't like it … but yes, I am enjoying it, Sir,' I admitted eventually.

'The people up there enjoy displaying themselves for others to watch, there is no reason for you to feel uncomfortable – everything here is consensual and for pleasure. If they didn't wish to perform then they would simply have sex in the privacy of their bedrooms,' he explained almost tersely making me wish I hadn't opened my mouth in the first place.

Seeing as Nathan seemed to be in a foul mood now his next move took me completely by surprise as he suddenly dragged me from my stool across onto his lap. I gasped in shock, but actually rather liked this new positioning as he sat me between his legs with my back to his front and began to slowly massage my waist.

Leaning in close to my ear, I felt him trail his lips briefly across the skin of my neck, almost sending me into an instant swoon. 'Is watching the show making you feel warm and wet inside your panties, Stella?' Nathan asked me, causing my swoon to evaporate and my eyebrows to shoot up in alertness. He wasn't about to initiate something sexual here was he? In public? Surely even Nathan wouldn't do that, would he? But the salacious and expectant tone of his voice certainly suggested so. Crikey, at least he wasn't annoyed with me any more I suppose.

Flushing beetroot red at the thought of getting intimate with Nathan in a public place I swallowed loudly again and then realised he'd asked me a question. To be truthful or not, that was the tricky thing. After his strop at my last little fib, I decided to go all out and be truthful. Nodding I heard a croaky voice, which was apparently mine. 'Yes, Sir.'

Next to my ear, Nathan growled softly, sending goosepimples rushing down my neck.

That was nothing though, he then proceeded to kiss and nibble around my exposed neck while his other hand disappeared below the table and cupped my groin though the thin material of my dress. *Holy fucking shit.* He was getting down and dirty with me in the middle of a bar. OK, so maybe we were set off to the side a little with a gauze curtain hiding some of our exploits, but still …

After getting me shamelessly aroused Nathan slowed his movements, settled his chin on my shoulder and instructed me to watch the show that was about to start. Grateful for the brief chance to catch my breath we both sat in silence, the only sound being our heavy, laboured breaths, as we watched a naked young woman enter the stage followed by an equally naked and already aroused man. Gosh, he was certainly keen.

The woman allowed herself to be tied to a long thin bench before the man began kissing and fondling her rather wanton body. She was moaning and writhing around in ecstasy within seconds, which seemed a little quick to me, even given the current situation. Maybe she was a good actress who liked to please the crowd. Quite apparently, one man wasn't enough for

147

this overzealous young lady though, because I then watched in open fascination as a series of men came onto the stage and pleasured her in one way or another. After the fifth man was done with her she moaned again and by this point I knew it must be real, there was no way any woman could endure all of the stimulation she had and not react. *I* was reacting and I wasn't even on stage.

A warning growl by my ear alerted me to the fact that I had been unconsciously wriggling in Nathan's lap, *oops*. But the show had got me more than a little hot under the collar so right now I either needed a release, or a distraction. Going for the latter, I turned away so I could see Nathan's profile next to me. 'Do you ever join in, Sir?' I kicked myself for the hint of jealousy in my tone and hoped Nathan hadn't picked up on it.

'No,' he said decisively, still staring at the stage and avoiding eye contact with me. 'I gave a series of demonstrations on the correct use of floggers and paddles once,' he added informatively as his grip tightened on my hips. Oh? We'd used a paddle once or twice, but never a flogger, interesting.

'If you were thinking you might like a session up on stage you can forget it. You are mine, Stella, no one else gets to watch you, let alone pleasure you.' His voice was icy cold, his grip even tighter on my hipbones, and once again, I found myself astounded by just how quickly his mood could change. Erratic or what? Allowing a small smile to creep onto my lips, I decided that mercurial or not, I quite liked his possessive statement about me.

My smile faded as I considered the idea of me being up on stage with all these people watching. I felt my stomach tense uncomfortably at the thought and decided I needed to set him straight on that matter … just in case he changed his mind in the future and wanted me to display myself, because that was not happening. *No way.*

'I wasn't thinking about going up there, Sir,' I replied quickly. 'I would hate to be looked at by all those strangers.' I tried to show my displeasure of the idea in my tone, but then I fell silent again as I noticed that the performers on stage had changed and a different man and women had begun to kiss and undress each other.

Ding, ding, round two.

Once again, I found that after watching the performance for a few minutes I was squirming in Nathan's lap almost uncontrollably. My unconscious movements weren't helping Nathan either, because the solid length of his erection was now pressing firmly against my lower back.

I couldn't decide if I was thrilled or horrified, but over the next few minutes Nathan began teasing me relentlessly by mirroring whatever was happening on the stage; if her nipple was tweaked Nathan tweaked my nipple through the fabric of my dress, if the man touched the woman between her legs, Nathan pulled my dress up and pressed between my legs with his dextrous fingers, it was like 4-D television, experiencing whatever I saw in front of me. Jeez, after just a few minutes I was panting like a rabid animal and squirming in his hands.

Nathan pushed gently on my hips and I dazedly followed his movements and stood up, my trembling fingers clutching the table in front of me trying to steady myself. Hah! Who was I kidding? I could have had concrete poured in my shoes and I still wouldn't be steady on my feet right now.

Reaching around me, Nathan extinguished the candle on the table with a hiss, removing the small trace of light and plunging our alcove into almost complete darkness. My mind was so fogged with lusty desire that without really realising it I found that Nathan had me fully bent forwards over the table in a position that no doubt left me wide open to him. I winced in embarrassment, just knowing that I must be soaking wet by now, not that he'd be able to see much in the darkness.

'Keep watching the show,' he murmured next to my ear and I discovered that I had unconsciously closed my eyes in an attempt at coping with my lust. Blinking against my hazy arousal, I watched as the guy on stage inserted not one, not two, but three fingers into the woman on the stage. True to form, Nathan proceeded to do the same to me and I very nearly dissolved on the spot. God, I was like one big, stretchy, melted ball of delicious arousal.

In front of me on the stage, the man laid himself down on

the padded bench and the women straddled him and mounted him in one swift movement that made my eyes pop open wider and the guy on stage to cry out in apparent shock. With no warning or other preparation Nathan suddenly pulled me back gently into his lap, and more shockingly, onto his waiting cock so that in one move he was completely sheathed within me.

Bloody hell! I hadn't even heard or felt him undoing his trousers, but quite evidently, he had because there was no mistaking the fact that he was now filling me to bursting point. Scrambled brain, that's what I had right now. I could barely concentrate on the performers on the stage, let alone on the deliciousness of what Nathan was doing to me as he started to slowly pump me up and down, but then I noticed the people on stage were joined by another man.

Interesting, I was just wondering what role he would play in the scene on stage when he began to massage the woman's breasts as she was writhing around on top of the first guy. OK, he was obviously just there to add a bit of interest. Jeez, this was like watching porn and partaking in it at the same time: how bad was that! Very bad, that's how bad.

I nearly giggled out loud at the ridiculousness of the situations that I seemed to get myself into these days, but my laughter died in my throat as I watched the stage and realised it might be about to get much worse.

Widening my eyes I watched as the breast man stepped away and begun to lube up his fingers and manhood. What the hell was he doing? The woman was already impaled on the other guy so there was nowhere for him to go … unless … oh God, I full on gasped when I realised was about to happen on stage, but then gasped even louder when I heard Nathan spit on his fingers behind me.

Oh no, no, *noooo*. This was something I hadn't done before and the thought of it instantly doused my current state of arousal. Nathan obviously picked up on my sudden tension, although seeing as he was buried balls deep inside me it would be hard for him not to I suppose.

'It's obvious that you have concerns about this area of sex, Stella, but as I said at the start of our agreement I like to test your limits every now and then. I've come to know you very well these last few weeks, you like to be tested, to be pushed, I can see that, you just won't admit it to yourself yet. Having said all that, if you wish me to stop simply say 'red' and I will.'

His words weren't particularly reassuring to me though and as the man on stage began to rub at the woman's exposed arsehole Nathan slowly began to do the same to me, finding the bunch of muscles at my tight rear entrance and rubbing his finger around them gently. *Fuck. Fuck. Fuck.* It was quite a confusing state to be in, because while my mind screamed no I had to admit that what he was doing actually felt rather nice. But it was the thought of more that terrified me.

'You are still tense, Stella, but you haven't said "red" yet …' Nathan sounded perplexed. 'If I assure you that the only thing going in here will be my little finger would that make you feel better?'

God yes, I nodded and exhaled a huge breath that fogged on the table below me and decided that after tonight I'd be adding another thing to my 'no' list on our contract. Bum sex? No thank you.

As the guy on stage entered the woman's well-lubed arse with his gigantic cock, I winced in sympathy for her, even though she seemed to be loving it, and then I waited expectantly as Nathan gently pushed the tip of one finger into me while still moving his cock in and out of my front hole. Talk about stuffed full.

'What colour are you?' Nathan asked gruffly, and I knew he was referring to my comfort levels and not my face, which was positively burning and must be redder than ketchup. Chewing on my lip, I gripped the table harder, but didn't seem to be able to bring myself to admit out loud that I enjoying what he was doing to me, it seemed so wrong … but surprisingly it felt fine, not painful at all, quite pleasurable in fact. Not that I had any future plans to upgrade his finger to anything larger, just one little finger was my limit.

Before I knew what was happening Nathan gripped my hips and pushed me forwards and away from him so abruptly that I was left lying on the table with my skirt up around my hips completely untouched by him like a discarded napkin, a sensation that left me feeling cold and bereft and wondering what the hell had happened.

Leaning down over me Nathan whispered in my ear in a deadly tone. 'If I ask you a question I expect an immediate answer.' He sounded as if he was speaking between gritted teeth, and I winced at my unerring ability to bring out the worst in him. 'You make me wait again and I shall simply walk away and leave you here,' he threatened. 'What is your colour?'

A mortification flush swept my already red cheeks, but I didn't keep him waiting a second time. 'Green,' I replied in a soft whisper.

'Are you certain?' he demanded hotly.

'Yes Sir ... green.' Almost instantly, Nathan's hands were on my hips again guiding me back towards his waiting cock and once he was firmly embedded in my tight channel, one of his fingers worked its way back to my rear hole and took up its illicit fondling again.

The combination of both my entrances being stimulated left me feeling surprisingly full and rather overwhelmed with pleasurable sensation, something I never thought would have come from the exploration of that most private of body parts, but amazingly as I felt myself driving towards an impossibly strong orgasm I had to admit that Nathan had been right when he said I liked my limits pushed.

'Nathan ... I'm going to come,' I murmured, forgetting myself and using his first name instead of 'Sir' as I squirmed desperately on the table. What made everything more intense was the fact that I was fully aware that I was possibly about to have one of the best orgasms of my life when just a few feet away on the other side of a gauze curtain were a bar full of people.

'As am I,' he informed me with a soft grunt. 'You'd best do it quietly, I forbid you to draw attention to yourself and cause other people to watch you as you climax. If you do I shall punish you when we get home and you will not enjoy it.'

His words were enough to finish me off and as Nathan continued to circle his throbbing cock inside me while simultaneously sinking his finger in and out of my rear hole I bit down on my own forearm and came with such force that my contractions seemed to instantly trigger Nathan's own silent release as I felt his warmth flooding inside me in a multitude of sharp thrusts.

Using several rolls of his very talented hips to ease me down from my climax, which quite frankly had been utterly sublime, Nathan eventually pulled out of me, cleaned me off with a hanky, righted both my clothes and his trousers, and then murmured something about me coping very well with new experiences, to which I merely grunted in response – I was too exhausted to speak at the moment.

As he stood he pulled a lighter from his pocket and re-lit the candle, slid open the gauze curtain, not that it had really given us much extra privacy, and then left it open as he disappeared to the toilets and then the bar to get us both a drink.

I noted with a snort as he walked away that Nathan seemed completely calm and able to walk normally, which pissed me right off, after that little sex-escapade I doubted my ability to even sit up straight at the moment, but after another moment of table recovery I pushed myself upright on the stool and thankfully managed not to fall off.

Still reeling from my brazen public sexual act I barely noticed the man that was standing against a column opposite me, in fact the first I really knew about him was when his broad figure blocked the narrow entrance to the alcove where I had been sat staring out blindly as I relived the details of my recent illicit tryst.

'Good evening. I don't believe I've seen you in here before.' Blinking rapidly as my trance was brought to a halt I looked up at the man now stood before me. I felt slightly dazed and didn't really want to be dealing with a stranger at this particular moment, but my inbuilt manners forced me to try and smile politely.

'No … it's kind of my first time,' I acknowledged with a nod. First time in a sex club, first time having sex in a sex club, first time having a finger up my … well, a blush bloomed on my cheeks, tonight really was a night of many firsts.

'Excellent.' the stranger replied, which I thought was an odd response, and his enthusiasm for my newness was a bit unnerving too. I felt marginally concerned by his apparent interest in me, and my concern only grew when he gave me a close inspection. I probably looked thoroughly well fucked at the moment, but decided that two could play that game so I also ran my eyes over him to try and suss him out. He looked to be in his late thirties and was very tall, broad, and rather muscular, almost too muscular for my tastes. My eyes widened as I looked at his arms, jeez, he had biceps like tree trunks. As for his face, he was probably as close to a vampire as a human could get – dark hair, dark eyes, pale skin, and good looks that would rival most of the customers present in the club tonight.

None of this appealed to me though, perhaps that was just because he was a bit too brutish for my tastes, or perhaps it had a little something to do with my growing obsession for a certain Mr Jackson and his handsome, tall, blond godliness.

'Are you here alone?' the big guy enquired. 'Perhaps you're looking for some company?' he added with a hopeful glint in his eye. Oh God, really? I could so do without this.

'Actually, I'm with someone,' I replied, wanting to put him off straight away. Thinking of Nathan, where the heck was he? Then with a roll of my eyes I realised he was probably washing himself in the toilets, obsessive-compulsive freak that he was.

'Really? And who are you with?' the guy asked in a tone that left no room for me to avoid answering. But how should I answer? Nathan had said that as we were in a club that catered directly for people of our lifestyle I could refer to him as 'Sir' – especially if I wanted to make him happy – and seeing as I'd already slipped up once and called him Nathan I decided to swallow my embarrassment and say what any good submissive would.

'I'm here with my master.' God, it felt weird to say that, and sounded even stranger out loud, but even though 'master' wasn't a term I ever called Nathan, it was apparently a perfectly acceptable response within the walls of Club Twist because the stranger in front of me nodded his understanding and gave me a broad and rather spectacular grin. OK, so he might not be my type exactly, but after that grin, I'd upgrade him to a brutish vampire guy worthy of any *Twilight* film.

'A sub, are you? How charming.' He sounded rather upper class, his words almost rolling from his tongue. Hiding a smirk I suspected his rather clichéd velvety tone was a deliberate 'charm them from their panties' approach, which had no doubt been used on numerous women before me, and I was swiftly proven right. 'Well, I have to say you've just made my night, I think you may be exactly what I'm looking for. Take a walk with me,' he ordered softly extending an arm to me. Bloody cheek! Who did he think he was?

My eyes widened in a look that I hope told him of my disbelief at his arrogant forwardness. He had effectively released my inner beast though, and I felt my annoyance levels rising, how dare he assume that just because I was a sub I would do whatever he bloody well wanted! Not to mention the fact that I'd clearly just said I was with someone and he was trying to steal me away which surely was against the code of dominants wasn't it? If, in fact, there was a code at all.

'No thank you. As I said before, I'm here with my master,' I repeated tartly, only just managing to hold my anger at bay in the hope that he would just go the hell away.

'Well he can't be much of a master if he's left you here all alone, little one. Wouldn't you rather come with me? I'll show you how a real dominant treats a sub as lovely as you,' he said with an annoying amount of gloating evident in his voice. God, this guy really was an arrogant piece of work.

'Dominic, I believe the lady said she's taken.' A cold voice interrupted, and as 'Dominic' turned his large body to see who it was that was interrupting him he unblocked the alcove entrance, allowing me to see an incredibly pissed-off Nathan glaring at the other man fiercely with his hands bunched around two glasses as if he might shatter them at any second. Even with Nathan looking ready to commit murder an involuntary smile flew to my lips at his return.

'Nathan?' Dominic said in surprise before turning back to me with an odd expression on his face. '*This* is your master?' he asked me incredulously.

'Yes,' I replied confidently. Bloody hell, Nathan looked ready explode on the spot. Quickly standing, I moved beside him in a show of my commitment and, after reliving him of the drinks, I placed them on the table, linked my hands in front of me and lowered my eyes as he liked. I also hoped that by doing this I might calm Nathan enough to stop him killing the big brutish guy, which at this moment was exactly what it looked like he wanted to do as the muscle on his jaw went into hyper drive, twitching and jerking like it was going to jump from his face.

'Haven't seen you in here for a while, Nathan, I didn't realise you were still on the scene.' Dominic murmured, holding out a hand towards Nathan for a handshake. Instead of reciprocating like I had expected, Nathan instead wound his hand around my waist and pulled me snugly against his side while he continued to shoot daggers at Dominic with his icy gaze.

I noted several points of interest here; one, I was damn glad I wasn't on the receiving end of his stare because it looked manic. Two, he had his arm around me which had never occurred before, but felt rather nice, and three, Nathan had quite clearly just made a claim over me in front of this other guy which thrilled me immensely.

'No offence meant, Nathan, I thought she was fair game, didn't realise she was with you,' Dominic said, not sounding the least bit apologetic and still looking at me like I was a piece of meat for sale. God, this guy really needed to learn some manners.

Not sure if I was allowed to speak, I found that I just couldn't help myself, this guy was such an arrogant arsehole and he really needed putting in his place. 'I told you I was with my master, how much clearer could I be?' Nathan would never have tolerated my tone if it had been directed at him, I knew this much, but my loaded question had been thrown towards Dominic and apparently Nathan wholehearted approved because not only did he give my waist an encouraging squeeze, but he then did something completely out of character – met my gaze and smiled at me broadly.

Wow – a real, no nonsense smile from Nathan. It was so stunning that my legs almost felt weak and I was immensely grateful for his arm around my waist keeping me upright. Good God, but this man could smile when he wanted. It was such a shame he didn't use it more often, although if he did I suspect women would be falling at his feet left, right, and centre.

A frown settled on my brows at my last thought; I only saw him at the weekends so for all I knew women *were* falling at his feet on a daily basis. This was a thought that I did not like one bit, but at the moment Nathan was smiling down at me looking so proud that I couldn't help but shelve my jealousy and smile shyly back before averting my gaze.

Without saying one more word to us, Dominic pursed his lips and then disappeared into the crowd, leaving Nathan and I alone at last. A sudden feeling of awkwardness came over me as I stood encased by Nathan's arm, and apparently he felt it too because he cleared his throat and then dropped his arm, leaving me feeling a little chilly even though it was excessively hot in the club.

'So who was that guy?' I asked in hopes of breaking the strange silence that had fallen over us now.

Nathan sneered and looked in the direction that Dominic had left in. 'One of the co-owners of this place. The guy behind the bar that introduced you to me, David Halton, is the original owner and used to run Twist as just a small bar from the premises next door, but then a couple of years ago this place came up for sale so he joined together with a few other investors, Dominic included, and expanded the bar into a club too. David likes to be front of house whereas the others like to take a back seat.' Nathan pushed my new drink towards me and set about finishing his. 'Drink up; I've had enough of this place for tonight.'

TWENTY-ONE – NATHAN

Running a hand through my hair, I scowled as I practically tugged a handful out and then tried to reassemble it into something resembling its usual order. I was feeling distinctly out of odds tonight and I couldn't really put my finger on why. That wasn't strictly true, actually: several things had pissed me right off in the last week that were no doubt contributing to my mood.

Firstly was last weekend when I'd gone to Club Twist with Stella, I'd thought it would be good for her to see other like-minded people, but in the end the only thing that had occurred was for me to get more and more fucking annoyed as various twats stared at her and ogled her body. *Fuckers*. It had taken every ounce of my self-control not to deck someone. She was with me for fuck's sake; they should keep their fucking eyes to themselves. Closing my eyes, I ground my teeth together as I remembered how Dominic had looked at her like she was his for the taking. *She was mine.* That was the last time we would be going there for a while, that was for sure.

The other thing that had pissed me off this week was the continuing issues at work. We'd lost another fucking contract to someone undercutting us, again by 18 per cent. Who the fuck was I kidding? Work was shit at the moment, but Gregory was on the case and I had every confidence he'd sort it.

No, if I was honest with myself then I could admit that all my issues were because of Stella. As well as attracting far too much male attention last weekend, she'd gone and topped up my anger towards her by getting an urgent phone call from work this morning. It was Saturday, my day with her, but she'd not thought twice about going into the fucking office for some weekend overtime.

So now I was sitting on my own like Billy No-mates, when really I should be doing something deliciously kinky with Stella. *Fuck it.* I was in such a bloody bad mood. I felt fidgety and far from my usual self.

Sighing, I picked up the phone next to me and dialled my brother. It had been a while since we'd met up for a beer, maybe a few late afternoon drinks with Nicholas would take my mind off Stella and all the kinky things I wanted to do to her but couldn't.

After exchanging brief pleasantries with Nicholas, I frowned and my eyes narrowed suspiciously at his tone. He was sounding decidedly perky, which was not a description that would usually apply to my stoic, withdrawn brother.

'What's made you so happy, Nicholas, you sound like you're grinning as you speak,' I asked, realising that I was actually scowling at my brother's apparent happiness. With my foul mood I think I had actually been hoping to find him in his usual dour mood to match my own melancholy.

There was a chuckle down the line from Nicholas and my eyes widened like saucers. A fucking chuckle? Really? My mood dropped another notch lower.

'If you must know, I've finally started sleeping with that woman I told you about,' he confessed, sounding rather smug.

Ah, OK so this was making a little more sense now. If there was one thing my brother and I had in common, it was our insatiable appetite for sex. That, and our preference for being dominant in the bedroom. 'Your piano student? Rachel, was it?' I asked, trying to remember what he'd told me about the woman he'd met a few weeks ago and offered some lessons to. My brother was a world famous concert pianist, not a piano teacher, so when I'd heard he'd offered her lessons I'd kind of assumed that he had an ulterior motive. Turns out I was right; his ulterior motive was sex.

'Rebecca. Yes, I'm still giving her lessons but things have developed physically between us. I have to say I'm surprised by how well it's going.' He sounded like he was grinning again, and in return I glowered. It was just as well we weren't on video call otherwise Nicholas would see just what a miserable git I was being today. Wasn't I supposed to be supportive and pleased for him?

'So as well as your student she's now your submissive? That's probably pushing the whole "naughty pupil and pervy teacher" thing a bit far don't you think?' I teased wickedly, my mood lifting slightly at the lovely kinky images that such a scenario would present.

'Rebecca's not my sub, Nathan, we've discussed my issues and we're working around them,' Nicholas explained cautiously and this time my scowl transformed to a complete look of shock. Not his submissive? What the hell was she then? With our fucked-up childhood, it had been easier for Nicholas and I to avoid the whole girlfriend thing, in fact both of us had started down the route of only getting involved with submissives and stuck to it. Well, I'd stuck to it, but apparently, my younger brother was now branching out.

Pausing I ran Nicholas' crazy words through my mind several times before finally finding my tongue. 'She's not your sub? Are you crazy?' I spat. OK, so that wasn't the most tactful of responses, but what the hell else could I say? Nicholas wasn't ready for this shit, he needed to realise what he was getting himself into before it was too late.

'This is none of your business, Nathan, Rebecca's different, she accepts me, I'm trying to be normal for a change.' Nicholas sounded pissed off with me, but I wasn't going to let it drop, this type of error would only lead to heartache for my brother in the long run.

'We're not capable of this type of relationship, Nicholas, it will never work, it's not how we were brought up,' I muttered through clenched teeth.

'Well maybe we were brought up wrong,' Nicholas snarled down the line at me. Snarled? At me? What the fuck was going on? Nicholas never got angry with me, I was his rock, his older brother; he looked up to me for Christ's sake.

'Our family life wasn't exactly normal, was it, Nathan? I know you can't see it but Dad was seriously fucked up,' Nicholas continued. Rubbing my forehead, I tried to ease the tension building there. I was going to get a mammoth migraine at this rate. Jesus, this was all so unexpected and certainly not what I'd expected when I called my brother this evening.

I cringed at my brother's mention of our father, but refused to allow his words to sink in. 'I don't want to talk about Dad, Nicholas, but he was our father, our role model, part of him is inside us both, brother, deep down you know it. You need to end this thing with her before one of you gets hurt.' By this point my words were being pushed through clenched teeth, how fucking stupid was Nicholas being? Surely he could see that there could be no long-term future in a 'normal' relationship for men like us with our fucked-up histories?

There was a tense silence where neither of us spoke and then with a sigh Nicholas was the first to break it. 'I'm playing a charity concert tonight, I need to go and practice. Goodbye, Nathan.' He hung up leaving me feeling even more unsettled than I had been to begin with. Well, as mood-lifting phone calls go that had been a complete fucking failure, hadn't it?

Later that night I heard a key in the door and jumped irritably to my feet standing in front of the door with my arms crossed and no doubt with my annoyance clearly evident on my features. My mood hadn't shifted in the slightest, my continued annoyance was partly due to the heated conversation I'd had earlier with my brother, partly because I'd just got off the phone with Gregory who had informed me that the issues with my company were still not fucking sorted, but mostly because Stella had said she'd only be in work for a few hours and it was nearly bloody six o'clock now, meaning I'd lost out on an entire one of our allotted days together.

Stella entered the apartment as usual, deposited her work bag by the door, hung her coat on the rack, and then turned to face me. As was her routine if I was around she then assumed my chosen position for her; head bowed with hands joined in front of her waiting expectantly. Fucking lovely. That pose nearly erased my foul mood with just one look at her, but then I remembered the whole great list of things that had fucked me off recently and my mood descended again.

'You're late,' I growled, not attempting to hide my irritation or the glower on my face, she should damn well know that I was pissed off.

'I know, I got stuck in a meeting, I'm sorry, Sir.' Stella explained softly in that tone of hers that usually soothed me, but not tonight. Tonight I was wound up tighter that a clock spring.

'I have told you how much I dislike lateness, Stella,' I reminded her sharply. In response, Stella nodded sagely, her eyes still remaining averted. God, she was good at the whole submissive thing, and she was great at avoiding eye contact with me, which made my life a whole hell of a lot easier. 'I don't expect this to happen again, do you understand?'

'Yes, Sir, sometimes it's unavoidable, though.' Seriously? That was how she wanted to play this?

My eyes narrowed and a grumble of annoyance escaped my throat as I raised my right hand in a pointing gesture, causing Stella to move immediately to my side just within touching distance. I could smell her perfume, slightly sweet and floral and enticing me to her, but I shook my head and clenched my fists tight to avoid reaching out and touching her. 'That's not the answer I want to hear, Stella,' I warned again in a low tone. 'You need to remember my expectations.' Damn right she did; I wasn't happy with her doing overtime in the first fucking place, and now to top it off she was late? It wouldn't be happening again, that was for sure. Maybe I'd switch her phone off next weekend when she arrived and damn the consequences.

'Yes, Sir,' Stella murmured. 'Perhaps you should help remind me,' she added a few moments later.

I sucked in a sharp breath at her words and salacious tone. This woman was like the ultimate submissive – she did everything she was asked, enjoyed the same things as I did in the bedroom but still kept me on my toes by occasionally throwing out a comment like that one. What exactly did she mean? I had a fairly good idea, but it seemed too good to be true … I needed to hear the words for myself.

'What would you recommend?' I asked, my earlier irritation suddenly subdued by a rush of excited anticipation from Stella's provocative tone. Christ, even my cock was joining in with my excitement and we hadn't even left the hallway yet.

'Well, I broke one of your rules ...' Stella left her sentence hanging but raised her eyes and made the briefest of eye contacts before lowering her gaze again.

My nostrils flared. Stella wanted to be punished. She wanted *me* to punish her. She had as good has asked for it, perhaps not in so many words, but it was enough of an invitation to get my blood pumping furiously around my body. I just needed to hear her say the words out loud ...

'You need to be disciplined for your lateness, Stella.' I murmured thickly, clenching my fists at my sides in an effort to maintain my control and hoping that she would give me the consent I was looking for.

Rolling her lips between her teeth she blinked several times and then nodded, 'Yes, Sir.' Her whisper was so slight I only just heard it, but it had been there, the words I had needed, and by God I certainly wouldn't let her down.

Lowering my voice, I stepped back distancing myself from her. 'Go to your room, undress, and sit on the bed. I'll teach you not to be late again,' I ordered in a cool tone that was the total opposite of my current feelings as my heart hammered erratically under my skin and my cock leapt about in my pants. Then I turned and walked away nonchalantly into lounge as if I couldn't care less that she was here, Jesus, it was the hardest thing I'd done in a long while.

It was difficult, no, nearly fucking impossible, but I made myself leave Stella hanging for 15 minutes before finally making my way to her room. Walking in with my eyes lowered I quietly closed the door behind me and then turned to see Stella sat on the edge of the bed with her eyes lowered and her hands joined in her lap.

Her skin was mottled with a fine spray of goosepimples and as I stepped closer I realised with a slight pang of guilt that she had probably got cold waiting naked for me for so long. Instead of allowing my guilt to bloom, a smirk curled my lips – I'd soon warm her up.

'I made you wait, Stella, just like you made me wait. Annoying, isn't it?' I murmured softly as I allowed my eyes to rove across her near perfect figure. Perfect for me anyway, with curves in all the right places and skin so soft and sweet I could almost taste it in my mouth already.

'Yes, Sir,' she answered softly. I watched in fascination as her breasts rose and fell when she spoke. They were perfect handfuls and my arms twitched at my sides with the effort of restraining myself. Her nipples were already hardened into peaks and I wondered if it were from excitement or the coolness of the room, but judging from the pulse I could see fluttering in her neck it was the former. Personally, I felt ready to burst at any moment, so that made two of us then.

Counting down from five to zero, I drew in several breaths through my nose to compose myself. Finally, I felt in control enough to reach out and run a hand through her beautifully soft hair. 'Are you going to make me wait in future, Stella?' I questioned as the strands slid between my fingers and fell in waves around her perfectly pert nipples. She really was pretty as a picture.

'I'll try not to, Sir,' Stella answered, causing me to frown and drop my arm. How dare she deliberately try to taunt me, didn't she realise that these were my rules and she needed to keep to them? I'd followed my father's fucking rules to the letter for the entirety of my childhood and Stella would damn well do it for me now. Roughly gripping her chin between my forefinger and thumb, I tugged. 'Stand up,' I ordered, noticing how my voice had unwittingly got far harsher at the thought of my father's iron will.

Obliging me immediately, Stella stood, but before she'd even got her balance properly, I gripped her hips, turned her round and pushed on her shoulder to bend her over the bed. 'Wait there,' I ordered, stepping to the chest at the end of the bed and opening the drawer where I kept my favourite toys. Pausing for a moment, I looked at Stella again; she had maintained her pose perfectly. Her back was arched downwards so that her shoulders and hips were thrust up, making her arse sit prominently waiting for my attention. A small sigh escaped my lips at just what a perfect sight she was.

Initially I selected the leather paddle and weighed it in my hand. The leather made a satisfyingly loud noise and although it tended to redden flesh initially, it didn't leave bruises. Not if you knew how to use it properly anyway, and I prided myself on my skill with these toys. My eyes flicked back to the contents of drawer; perhaps tonight I could use something just a little different, Stella had asked to be punished after all.

Kicking the drawer shut once I had selected an appropriate tool, I stalked back around to Stella's prone form and with no warning at all slapped her firmly across the backside with a suede flogger. This one was a particular favourite of mine: 13 suede strips hung from the handle and each had a tiny little knot tied in the end to add a little extra bite if you so chose. Tonight I wanted it to.

The slapping noise was louder than expected and seemed to reverberate off the walls. Perhaps I'd gone a little hard with that first strike, but as Stella arched her back and gripped the duvet in fisted hands she let out a cry that was definitely pleasure induced. Watching in satisfaction, I saw the faint lines begin to appear on her left buttock as the blood rushed to the surface, leaving it glowing a soft pink colour. Unable to resist I reached down and rubbed it gently with my hand, loving how Stella pushed herself into my touch.

As distracting as her warm buttock was I needed to stay focused on my objective. Swallowing, I calmed myself again. *I am in control.* 'I'll ask you that question again, Stella. Are you going to make me wait in future?'

'It depends how busy work is, Sir.' she answered between gasped breaths.

Gritting my teeth, I closed my eyes. She was always so fucking honest! The things this woman did to me! Deep down I knew this was her way of taking a tiny bit of control by deliberately trying to rouse me, and it worked every time. God, the effect she had on me when she was defiant like this! It just made me want to fuck her into submission until she begged me to stop. Delicious images of me buried balls deep in Stella filled my mind, but I pushed them aside; there would be plenty of time for that later.

The flogger travelled almost silently through the air as I brought it down on Stella's other buttock, landing with the same satisfying sound. Stella threw her head back and let out a soft mewling sound that made my groin tighten instantly as I recognised her purr as a sign that she was enjoying herself. I couldn't help but grin to myself – she really was delightfully kinky – we were such a good match. Regardless of how great a pairing we made, Stella was still deliberately winding me up, which pissed me off, so I made sure that the next two strokes I landed were harder than the first, using those little knots to my advantage to add some extra sting for her.

Standing back, I admired my handiwork for a second before leaning over her back so my lips were brushing her ear lobe.

'It may have come to your notice that I don't like the answers that you are giving me, Stella. It makes me angry that you think so little of my rules. I'll ask you one more time.' With deliberate slowness, I ran my teeth around the rim of her ear, teasing the sensitive flesh with my tongue until I felt her shudder and lean into my touch. 'Will you ever be late arriving here again?'

'I will try my best not to be, Sir.' Her voice was breathy now and I guessed that she was loving every minute of this little scene just like I was. We really were so compatible in the bedroom.

'Oh dear, Stella. That really wasn't the answer I wanted,' I breathed harshly next to her ear before sitting myself on the bed and dragging her across my lap. Her red arse was just too tempting to waste on a flogger now; I needed skin-to-skin contact with it.

Using the heel of my hand in between her shoulder blades, I pressed until Stella's chest and face were against the duvet, stilling her, and then placed my free hand on her behind. A groan escaped my lips, it was so hot to touch that I very nearly flipped her onto the bed and took her there and then. Dragging breaths in through my nose I struggled for a second or two to calm myself. *I am in control.*

A quick countdown from 5 to 0 focused me enough to continue. 'You will not be late for me again, understand?' I demanded.

'I'll try,' she whispered against the cotton duvet. Still the wrong answer, she really was being a little temptress tonight. My hand rose up and then slapped down on her naked bottom hard enough to make Stella yelp and tense up across my lap. Beneath her my cock had leapt to full attention and was painfully constricted by my trousers, only adding to the overall sensation of this experience.

'You will not be late,' I stated again. 'Do you understand?' I was grinding the words out between gritted teeth now, half loving this little game while at the same time realising that Stella's deliberate provocation was seriously pushing me towards losing it completely.

'I don't want to lie to you Sir, I can't guarantee that I'll never be late.' Fuck, her honesty at times like this was incredibly endearing, even if it was downright frustrating, I thought with a shake of my head.

Finally letting the tightly wound spring inside me snap I let Stella have a further six hard slaps across her behind, leaving me almost as breathless as she was. I could feel her chest heaving against my thighs from the exhilaration and felt the palm of my hand beginning to burn. Looking at my reddened hand my cock pulsed again and I knew I wouldn't last much longer with Stella's naked, well-spanked body lying across me.

'You have one more chance to answer correctly, Stella,' I murmured ominously, rubbing across her backside with gentle fingers this time. The calm before the storm.

Between jagged breaths, Stella turned her head towards me. 'I won't be late again, I promise, Sir!' she cried in a breathy tone. Apparently, she'd understood that I had taken about as much teasing as I could cope with. Thank fuck for that because I was seriously at breaking point now.

'Good girl.' I let out a relieved sigh. Soothing her glowing buttocks with my palm, I ran my fingers in a teasing trail down and around her thighs to relax her, before finally slipping them between her slightly parted legs to reach around and see if she was wet for me. Christ, she was sopping. I closed my eyes and drew in a breath through flared nostrils as I shook my head in disbelief, the woman had just taken a serious spanking from me and she was dripping wet from it.

'Ahhhh …' Stella let out a sigh as my finger made contact with her clit. Then, pressing her elbows into the mattress, she tilted her hips backwards to increase the pressure on her sweet spot. A smile curved my lips, she always surprised me with just how keen she was in the bedroom. God she was so refreshingly insatiable.

Seeing as Stella had pleased me by taking her punishment so well I decided to reciprocate with just a bit of pleasure back. Increasing the pressure and speed of my fingers, I brought Stella close enough to a climax that I felt her body begin to tense before I stopped abruptly and flipped her onto her back.

Flushed cheeks and wide needy eyes greeted me, her frustration visible in the way she squirmed below me, arching her hips off the mattress and moaning softly, but still she remained silent with her eyes averted as I always requested. *I am in control.* But only just; at this moment, with Stella writhing with need below me, it was the hardest thing not to plunge inside her welcoming warmth, but I didn't.

Instead, giving her body just enough time to come down from her near orgasm I then replaced my fingers with my mouth and began my sensual torture all over again, licking up and down her moist folds, circling my tongue around her swollen clitoris before finally taking it in between my teeth and tugging gently until I felt her building to a release, before once again stopping.

I was being such a git tonight. Standing back, I watched as Stella's hands contorted in the duvet gripping it and bunching it up around her, as her eyes squeezed shut in frustration. 'Please … Sir,' she begged.

Ah, Stella begging, the sound was like music to my ears. Not that I'd give in to it, but it was still fucking satisfying to know I had so much power. Several seconds later, when she had once again dropped away from her climax, I began my attentions again. After mere minutes, just like the last time, I abruptly stopped my ministrations and glanced up at her. From my position between her legs, I caught her down turned gaze and treated her frustrated and flushed face to a wicked, dark smile. 'Seeing as you made me wait earlier I decided I should make you wait for your orgasm just a little longer, Stella. Kneel on the floor,' I demanded softly, rising from the bed and stepping back to give her room.

Watching in amusement, I noticed that Stella was flushed from head to foot and struggling to stand on her apparently wobbly legs. It never failed to make me feel smug when I saw how much I could affect her. The thought that she had a similar effect on me fleetingly entered my head, but seeing as it wasn't particularly pleasant to consider my personal weaknesses, I briskly pushed it aside.

'On your knees,' I reminded her again as she swayed unsteadily in front of me. Without further prompting, I watched as Stella sank to her knees in front of me and joined her hands in her lap to indicate she was ready for her next instructions. Stella, submissive, ready and kneeling in front of me – this was my favourite view *ever*.

'Fuck me with your mouth,' I instructed crisply, knowing I wouldn't last long in my current state, but not caring any more. I was dragged from my selfish thoughts but the surprising sight of a small smile tilting the corners of Stella mouth as she immediately reached for the button of my trousers. Wow, I knew Stella enjoyed giving me blowjobs, she'd shared this much with me in the past, but I was surprised by her pleased reaction today given how frustrated she must be feeling at her own lack of release.

Before I knew it, Stella had freed my straining erection and was palming it in her soft hand. Christ, that felt good. My head dropped back for a second and I closed my eyes before forcing myself to get control and watch her. I loved watching her pleasure me.

Lowering her mouth, Stella twirled her tongue around the tip of my penis like it was a lollipop before dragging her lips down to the base and back up again in a tortuously slow movement. God she was so damn good at this. Finally, when I thought I was going to grab her head and shove it against me, she took me fully into her mouth and her warmth and suction nearly made me lose it there and then.

Stella slipped her free hand around the base of my erection

and began squeezing at the same time as sucking me in a hard demanding beat, her cheeks hollowing out as she seemed to pleasure me almost greedily. Fuck, the sight of Stella clearly enjoying herself made me lose my last thread of control and I let out a groan as I came in her mouth in huge hot spurts that felt like they would go on forever.

Remaining in a kneeling position at my feet, Stella continued to massage my spent cock gently for several more seconds easing me down from my climax before finally releasing me and sitting on her heels expectantly. Jesus, even after such an explosive climax I was still half-erect and practically ready to go again.

Trying to regain control of myself after such an incredible experience I pushed my needy cock back into my trousers ignoring how much it wanted me to push Stella back and take her, then I did up my zip and reached forwards to stroke the top of her hair.

'Lay on the bed, you may get under the covers if you're cold,' I instructed softly while tucking my shirt back in. 'I have a small amount of work to do, I may come back to give you some release if I have time. Don't touch yourself, when you climax it will be because I make you. Do you understand?'

'Yes Sir.' Stella murmured climbing into bed and pulling the duvet around herself.

Stepping towards the bed, I tucked the duvet tightly around her before gripping her chin and pulling her face up to meet mine. 'Why am I making you wait for your orgasms, Stella?' I asked quietly.

'Because I was late and made you wait, Sir,' she replied softly, a hint of her frustration evident in the remaining flush on her cheeks and the small frown creasing her delicate brows. Good, my technique was working, she'd think twice before being late for me again.

'Exactly. Next time there's a chance that you're going to be late, remember this,' I advised before forcing myself to leave the room.

I was being particularly harsh on Stella tonight. I knew this much, but I wasn't entirely sure of the reasons why. Striding into the kitchen, I poured myself a glass of red wine and took a sip of its smoothness. My eyebrows tweaked together into a frown as I tried to remember the last time I'd managed to exercise such control over the urge to take a woman. Jesus, I had desperately wanted to fuck Stella just now, so much so that even the amazing blowjob she'd given me hadn't taken the edge off my need and even now, my erection still pulsed inside my trousers as if to prove the point.

Sipping my wine, I wandered through to the lounge and selected an armchair near the panoramic windows. Leaning back, I let out a sigh as I gazed out across the dimming London skyline. I'd lied to Stella, I didn't have any work to do tonight, I had just wanted to make her wait a little bit longer before I went back in there and screwed her brains out. Fuck, I was such an arsehole. Trying to work out why I was being so irrationally harsh I laid my head back and closed my eyes. The only reason I could think of was my recent stress. That and her deliberate teasing of me that had wound me up no end. In fact, I was now suspicious that she'd even been late on purpose just to torment me. Christ, I was getting paranoid.

Normally I liked her teasing and mild defiance, she never pushed it too far and was always careful to respect my dominance, but tonight for some reason it had irritated me.

Pondering this for a few minutes the only other reason I could come up with for my mood was that perhaps I was still harbouring a lingering annoyance from my call with Nicholas earlier. Repeatedly running the conversation through my mind I still couldn't get over how stupid he was being. Blinking back from my thoughts and realising that my conversation with my brother was probably the main reason for my irritable state I glanced guiltily at the clock and saw that I'd been sitting drinking for nearly 45 minutes. Chewing on the inside of my lip, I grimaced: that meant I'd made poor Stella wait for three-quarters of an hour. Shaking my head, I saw the sun had now completely set over London and lights were flicking on across the city as night began. It had been long enough. Standing up I refilled my glass before pouring one for Stella and making my way back to her bedroom.

Should I knock? Nah, this was my house and Stella was my submissive. Pushing the door open with my foot I entered and then kicked it shut behind me. Glancing at the bed I saw the side lamp was on and Stella was still awake. For a change, she was breaking my rule and looking straight at me almost reverently.

'I didn't think you were coming back,' she murmured quietly, sounding like a lost child. I winced at the hurt tone to her voice and felt like a complete shit for making her wait so long, deciding that on this occasion, I'd let her off for not using 'Sir' in the bedroom.

'May I join you?' I asked, to which Stella immediately nodded. Good, she might be a little hurt emotionally, but she still wanted me. Remaining quiet, I placed the wineglasses on the bedside table and silently began to remove my clothes as she watched with parted lips and growing heat in her expression. Oh yeah, I still had it.

'You were very angry with me for being late ... Sir,' she commented softly, adding my title quietly a second or so later.

'Yes I was,' I conceded, feeling another slice of guilt for my earlier treatment of her. Guilt? I never felt guilty over my actions, what the hell was this woman doing to me? Mind you, I had been pretty mean, orgasm denial was frustrating enough anyway, but I'd brought her close to climax what, three or four times? She must feel like an unexploded bomb right now.

'*Was*,' she said hopefully, picking up on my wording. 'Does that mean you aren't mad any more?'

'No. Not any more,' I acknowledged with a nod. I wouldn't apologise, though; Stella knew what she was getting into from the start with me, and apologies weren't something I did. 'Now, I think you might need some relief,' I commented lightly as I lowered myself onto the bed. 'Assuming you've followed my rule and haven't touched yourself.' Interestingly a blush bloomed on Stella's cheeks and I raised an eyebrow. 'Stella? Have you broken yet another of my rules?' I asked in a deadly soft tone.

Staring at her mouth I saw Stella purse her lips as she shook and nodded her head simultaneously, making it blindingly obvious that she was hiding something from me. Lowering my eyebrows, I flashed her my firmest look and almost immediately saw her quail and give me an apologetic shrug.

'I rubbed myself a little bit, Sir,' she admitted, flushing even redder.

Touching herself? I felt an unnecessary flare of jealousy towards her fingers and my eyes narrowed further as I crawled higher up the bed so I was sat right next to her. Gripping the edge of the blanket under her chin, I pulled back the duvet roughly to reveal her naked body. 'I didn't come, I swear!' Stella yelped with wide eyes.

'I see.' For some reason I believed her. 'Why did you do it?' I asked as I picked up her right hand and rubbed my thumb gently across her knuckles.

'I was ... it was throbbing, Sir.' Stella conceded weakly, dropping her eyes again. Yes, it probably would have been after my little teasing session.

'But you didn't come?' I enquired, lifting her hand to my lips and placing a kiss on the palm.

She looked confused by my oddly gentle actions, apparently wondering when I was going to lose it and go mad at her for breaking my rule, but I wasn't going to flip out again tonight; after realising I'd been too harsh earlier I was now intent on some pleasure for us both. Perhaps with a bit of mild teasing thrown in too. 'Stella, did you come? Tell me the truth?'

'No. I promise. You know I never lie to you, Sir,' she added.

This was true. As far as I knew, Stella was always completely honest with me, even if it meant she took more of a punishment like earlier. Her complete and utter integrity was one of her defining qualities, and something that I respected a great deal.

Shifting my grip to her wrist, I sucked one of Stella's fingers into my mouth and enjoyed a moment of running my tongue around it. 'Nope, not that one,' I murmured, before placing the next finger in my mouth. I repeated this process until I put her index finger into my mouth and tasted the slightly salty, musky tang of her bodily fluids. Looking up at her, I grinned darkly.

'Ah-ha,' I said around her finger, once again running my tongue the length of the digit. 'This is the one you used to touch yourself, isn't it?' I asked softly.

Apparently shocked by how light-hearted my tone had become – it was shocking, I was rarely this playful – Stella looked up at me with wide eyes, smiled shyly, and then nodded. 'I thought so, I can taste you,' I added, sucking her finger harder and giving it a little bite. Removing her hand, I rubbed my thumb over the small indentations where my teeth had been. 'That's to remind you not to touch yourself unless I say so,' I told her with another darker smile breaking on my lips as I decided that I rather liked marking her as mine.

Placing her hand down near her groin, I straightened up and made myself comfortable against the headboard. 'Show me how you rubbed yourself.'

Stella frowned, and in return, I smiled, she was obviously embarrassed by my demand. 'It can be embarrassing to talk about sex, or do something sexual when your partner simply watches, but Stella, look how much the idea of watching you excites me,' I explained, jerking a nod down at my straining erection. As if on cue it jerked up against my belly expectantly, and as I glanced back at Stella, I saw a soft smile on her lips as she looked at my arousal. Yeah, I often grinned when I eyed my big boy too. Someone upstairs had been generous when creating me because I was pretty lucky in that department.

'You must have been very frustrated, I bet it felt good to touch yourself a little bit, go on show me what you did,' I coaxed her, placing her hand even lower on her belly in assistance. Thankfully, my persuasion had worked this time and with a small clearing of her throat Stella averted her eyes and began to stroke herself. Greedily I watched as her finger dipped between her folds only to come out glistening with her arousal as she moaned softly.

Christ, it suddenly felt warm in the bedroom. Really fucking warm. Swallowing, I watched Stella fondle herself for a few more seconds before my composure cracked and I leapt on her. Literally, like a caged tiger suddenly released. Time to relieve her frustration. Not to mention mine.

TWENTY-TWO – STELLA

Glancing at the clock, I was shocked to see that it was 2.30 a.m. Shaking my head I smiled to myself. Two thirty, and Nathan had only just finished getting his fill of me for the night. Or should that be morning? A broader grin spread on my lips at the thought. Blimey, that had been a sex marathon and a half; perhaps I should turn up late to Nathan's more often if that was the reaction it got from him.

Rolling over towards his warm body I barely had time to blink before I registered that Nathan was up and gone from the room with a curse. Then it was another second or so until I could co-ordinate my ears to realise that there was a huge commotion going on somewhere outside the bedroom.

Bloody hell! Burglars! Surely it must be, it was two frigging thirty in the morning who else could it be? Jumping up I wrapped a sheet around myself and half tripped, half stumbled my way after him before realising that I'd be absolutely no help to him wrapped in a sheet. Cursing I dropped the sheet and quickly yanked on his discarded T-shirt before high tailing it out of the room.

My heart was hammering erratically in my chest, but as I reached the hallway, the scene by the front door was not what I had expected at all. Nathan wasn't fighting off some intruder as I had expected, nope, before me I watched as Nathan was stood frozen to the spot clad only in his boxer shorts staring helplessly at an agitated man who looked startlingly similar to himself. The man must surely be related to Nathan because apart from his dark, wavy hair the two could practically be twins.

Grabbing at his hair, the mystery man started swinging helplessly around on the spot crying and grimacing and uttering nonsensical sentences to a dazed Nathan who looked like he was chewing on his lip hard enough to break the skin.

The only words of his rant that I caught were 'Rebecca', 'gone', 'crazy', 'cane', and a huge string of fiery expletives. Clearly, something major had happened involving someone called Rebecca.

Then before my eyes, the man dropped to his knees, shaking, sobbing, and growling as if in great pain, followed shortly by Nathan, who to my astonishment simply wrapped himself around the guy and pulled him to his chest, trying to soothe him by rubbing his back and murmuring soft words I couldn't hear.

Christ, this was a show of emotion I had never experienced or expected to see from Nathaniel Jackson. He obviously cared a great deal about this guy and I suddenly felt as if I might be intruding on a hugely personal moment. There was no might about it: as I watched Nathan rocking the distraught man in his arms, I knew I *was* intruding on a hugely personal moment. As if reading my mind, he chose that exact moment to look up and uncharacteristically catch my eye. Nathan shot me a scowling glance before tipping his chin towards the bedrooms in a sign for me to leave him to it. I nodded my understanding, but as I turned he spoke. 'In fact, get dressed, Stella, you should leave.' Glancing back at him in surprise, I saw that he had already dismissed me and was once again intently focused on the other man.

Walking back to the bedroom, I felt the adrenaline rush from earlier leave my body and be replaced by a slighted feeling from Nathan's cold dismissal of me. It was clear that something major had occurred to Nathan's friend, brother, whatever he was, but I still would have expected him to treat me with a little more respect than just ordering me to leave.

I stopped dressing abruptly and closed my eyes on a grimace. *Bugger*, I was getting too attached to him, wasn't I? Allowing girly fantasies of Nathan as a knight in shining armour to cloud my view of things, but this was no fairy tale and he was certainly no knight, he was my dominant who fucked me at the weekends, end of story.

My posture slumped and I collapsed into a chair, resting my

face in my hands and breathing heavily. From the ache in my chest, it was suddenly shockingly clear that I no longer just thought of Nathan as my weekend sex guy. Shit. What a mess. Huffing out an irritated breath at my own stupidity I pushed my wayward hair from my face and jumped up, dressing in record time so I could leave a place where I was no longer wanted.

Returning to the lounge, I was intent on slipping out if possible, but found that Nathan and the man were now both standing and near the door, thwarting any ideas I had of a stealthy escape.

Chewing on my lip as I quietly made my way up the corridor, I watched Nathan carefully and saw the tension obvious in his bunched shoulders. He didn't notice my approach. Instead, his eyes were fixed on the mystery guy who seemed to have got himself marginally under control now, even though he still looked terrible and had blood red eyes from crying.

It was odd, as stressful as this situation was I couldn't help but notice that Nathan had no issues with full eye contact with this man at all, meeting his gaze boldly and continuously. Interesting.

They were talking softly but as I got closer, I overheard Nathan's last sentence. 'Stay here tonight, Nicholas; it's Sunday tomorrow; we can spend the day chilling here, you can talk if you want. I'll send Stella home. I can work from home next week so stay as long as you need. Maybe after work one night next week we can go for some drinks and talk once you've calmed down.'

As I heard Nathan refer to the man as 'Nicholas', it all fell into place for me. I'd been right; they were related. This man was Nathan's brother, Nicholas. A couple of years ago I'd been reading some crappy work magazine and it had featured an article on Nathaniel Jackson Architecture and how both the Jackson brothers had hit the top of success in their fields, Nathan in industry, and Nicholas for skill with musical instruments. If memory served me correctly, which it might not have because it was the middle of the frigging night and I was knackered, Nicholas was famous for his piano playing.

Glancing again at the brothers I noticed that although he looked marginally more composed, Nicholas' hands were shaking and he was chewing on the inside of his lip like mad. Similar agitation habits to his brother then, I noted with a raised brow.

Finally seeing my approach Nathan briefly flicked a glance at me then shuffled awkwardly on his feet. 'Stella, this is Nicholas, my brother.' He indicated between us with his hand. 'Nicholas, this is Stella, my sub.' I winced at the introduction, then blushed. It might be true but it still sounded strange out loud to be referred to as a 'sub'. In fact, why did he even have to say 'sub' at all? He could just have said, 'This is Stella,' and left it at that. Although thinking about how blunt Nathan usually was when it came to conversation it could actually have been a hell of a lot worse I suppose, he might have given a more full definition that would have left me cringing even more ... 'Nicholas, this is Stella. Stella enjoys light bondage, rough sex, and last week she let me stick my finger up her arse while in a nightclub full of people ...' A huge blush heated my cheeks. OK, so being introduced as his sub was a hell of a lot better than *that* description. Sub or sex slut? Jeez, what the hell was I doing with my life when stuff like this was actually a consideration for me?

Placing a light hand on my back Nathan then guided me towards the door indicating that he wanted me gone. I hid my upset from Nathan by keeping my eyes averted, but I couldn't hide it from myself and my stomach roiled and twisted uncomfortably as we reached the door.

Nathan stopped just short of the door and turned to me, but I stared at his bare feet not happy at all at how my body was reacting to his sudden dismissal of me. 'I need to spend some time with my brother, he's had a bit of a crisis tonight,' he said in way of apology, although to be fair I'd have had to be blind and deaf not to figure that much out on my own. 'Nicholas' driver, Mr Burrett, is downstairs, he'll take you home,' Nathan said before pausing thoughtfully. 'You'll come next weekend?' he asked, apparently wondering if I would show after being chucked out tonight.

To be honest I'd been asking myself the same question, but, as tempted as I was to take my mood out on him, it was obvious Nathan needed to help his brother so I resisted the urge to be snarly with him and decided not to jump to any rash decisions either. It was the middle of the night after all, and I was functioning on barely any sleep.

'Yep. I'll see you next Friday. I hope your brother is OK,' I mumbled as I stood waiting for him to open the door. An awkward moment hung between us, Nathan never saw me out at the end of our weekends, normally when Monday morning came around he had either already gone to work or was ensconced in his office as I left. We both loitered, him looking uncomfortable and me feeling like a teenager on a date, would he kiss me goodbye? I soon got my answer as Nathan opened the door and stood back. 'Close the door behind you,' he murmured giving me one last look before turning back to Nicholas.

No goodnight kiss, then. Not that I'd really expected one. My abrupt departure from Nathan's left me seriously thinking about exactly what I was doing in this 'thing' with him, and as I did the mortifying walk of shame past the night watchman in the lobby of his swanky apartments I'd never felt quite so much like a used and discarded sex thing in all my life. Maybe it was time to do more than just walk home, maybe it was time to walk away for good.

TWENTY-THREE – NATHAN

After I'd seen Stella out, I jogged to my bedroom to grab a pair of tracksuit bottoms and pull on something to cover my chest. I wasn't exactly sure what the fuck was wrong with Nicholas, but his appearance on my doorstep in the middle of the night looking like death warmed up had certainly scared the shit out of me.

Grabbing a T-shirt, I had it halfway over my head when I noticed it was warm against my face. Frowning, I sniffed it and realised it must have been the one Stella had just been wearing. Instead of getting pissed off that she was again wearing my clothes without asking I couldn't help but sniff the cotton again and enjoy the faint smell of her that lingered on the fabric.

As much as I would have loved to lose myself in Stella's scent, preferably accompanied by her lithe little body, I knew that ship had sailed, I'd sent her home, not very politely either, a realisation that had me chewing on my lower lip in regret. Shaking my head, I practically snarled in annoyance at myself. She was my submissive for fuck's sake, misplaced feeling of guilt shouldn't be affecting me right now when what I really needed to do was get to the bottom of what ever had upset my brother.

When I returned to the lounge I felt my stomach twist with apprehension, Nicholas was sat in total darkness, highlighted only by the moon shining in through my huge, glass wall. Sighing, I shook my head. Whatever had happened had seriously messed him up; in fact, I hadn't seen my brother this distraught for years.

I clicked on a lamp and watched as Nicholas leaned himself forwards and rested his elbows on his knees so he could hold his head in his hands. I couldn't see his face, but I was pretty sure he was crying again and didn't want me to see. I ran a hand through my hair and scratched at the back of my neck as I considered what to do. Fuck, I was no good at this type of thing, where the hell did I start?

Remaining silent, I padded across to him and took a seat on the wooden coffee table directly in front of his armchair. Close proximity was probably a good start; it would make him feel more supported. My eyes ran over him – he was wearing a crumpled grey T-shirt that was totally at odds with his smart trousers, ones I recognised as his concert suit because they had a line of black silk running down the side crease. It seemed he'd pretty much come here straight from his concert tonight.

'Right then, Nicholas, tell me what happened,' I murmured. Hopefully he'd do most of the talking and I could just do my best attempt at being a supportive brother.

Nicholas was silent for so long I thought he hadn't heard me so I repeated my question with a little more force. 'Nicholas, tell me what happened.' Then, before I knew what had hit me, Nicholas had reared up from his chair, gripped my T-shirt by the collar and forced me back on the coffee table with a roar. '*You*, Nathan! *You* fucking happened!' he screamed, a manic expression on his face as he shook me so violently that the back of my head bounced off the coffee table several times.

What the hell had I done? *Fuck*, I'd not seen him so crazy for years. Back when we were teenagers and dealing with the aftermath of Nicholas' attempted suicide he would sometimes get mad, rampage around the flat for a few minutes smashing stuff, but then completely deflate and cry for hours. He was so insular and quiet at the time, never talking about what had happened or how he felt that I suppose it had been his way of letting off steam.

Assuming that tonight's outburst was a similar venting tactic I forced myself to stay limp and calm as Nicholas discharged his stress until I eventually felt his grip loosen above me. Finally, he let go and slid to the floor next to the table where I heard several quiet sobs mix with his heavy breathing.

Sitting up I rubbed at my head with a wince. That would

definitely bruise tomorrow. Then I looked to Nicholas to see if he wanted to speak yet. He was sat hugging his knees to his chest and still staring at the floor. 'I hurt her, Nathan. I really fucking hurt Rebecca,' he whispered thickly. So this was to do with his piano student and now girlfriend, Rebecca. The skin on my neck prickled as his words sunk in. Fuck, what the hell did he mean? Hurt emotionally or hurt physically? Having just experienced a small shot of his anger just now I suddenly got a very bad feeling in my gut.

'Nicholas, is she OK? Where's Rebecca now?' I asked urgently.

Nicholas ignored me, speaking as if I wasn't even there. 'When I spoke to you on the phone before my concert you said I shouldn't date her ... said we couldn't do relationships like that.' He paused, running a shaky hand through his sweat slicked hair. 'It got me thinking about Dad and all the shit he put me through and I thought maybe you were right, maybe I am like him, so after the concert I called Rebecca and finished with her.' His hair got a full on tug this time as if he actually wanted to yank it from his scalp, and I winced. 'But Rebecca wouldn't accept it. She bloody well turned up at my house! It was the middle of the fucking night and she got in a cab with some stranger and came to my house! I was so fucking mad with her.'

None of this was easing my concern about Rebecca's wellbeing so I tried again to establish exactly how Nicholas had 'hurt' Rebecca. 'You were confused and mad, I get that, Nicholas, but what happened to Rebecca? Where is she?'

'I told her what you said about how I was incapable of relationships and that she was better off without me but she just wouldn't leave it be. *She's. So. Fucking. Stubborn.*' He was grinding the words out now, the muscles on his jaw going into hyper-drive as they twitched and tensed. 'I guess I flipped out, I don't really know what happened ... it's pretty blurry ... but somehow I ended up in the spare room with her and I grabbed a cane ...'

Oh fuck – no. My heart almost stopped in my chest at the implication of my brother's words. The night that Nicholas had tried to kill himself had been because our father had beat him unconscious with a cane. Is that what he'd done to Rebecca?

'Christ, Nicholas … is she OK? Is Rebecca OK? Do I need to make some calls?' My mind was rapidly running through all the contacts I had who might be able to help me out if Nicholas had done some real damage to Rebecca. I had several friends who were doctors who could help if she was injured … Fuck … what if it was worse? Jesus, when I'd told him not to date her I had meant finish with her, not beat the shit out of her. What if Nicholas had really lost it? My back started to sweat profusely as my mind raced through options. I knew at least one trusted solicitor who owed me a favour …

'Rebecca left me shortly afterwards … she's gone home, Nathan,' Nicholas murmured thickly.

'She's OK?' I demanded.

'She's not OK, but she's not dead if that's what you mean,' he confirmed grimly. 'She's furiously mad and massively disappointed with me and she's going to have some bruises tomorrow, but she's basically fine.'

My back sagged with relief at this news, thank fuck for that. For a few minutes there, I thought I was going to be dealing with the aftermath of something far worse than a bruised arse.

Nicholas was frantically tugging at his hair again, his eyes wild and darting around endlessly. 'I drew blood, Nathan, *I fucking drew blood.*' Suddenly as if remembering something Nicholas began to look agitatedly at his trousers, searching across the fabric in the dim light of the lamp. A scrambled yelp left his throat and then Nicholas jumped to his feet. 'Fucking hell!'

He practically ripped his trousers off, I assume because he found some of Rebecca's blood there, and flung them across the room before collapsing on the sofa and staring at me.

'What the hell have I done, Nathan? Why did you tell me to finish with her?' His voice no longer held the anger of earlier, now he simply seemed to be pleading for answers that I couldn't really give him.

'Nicholas, I'm sorry things worked out this way. Christ, I never meant for this shit to happen, but basically you've done the right thing, the way we grew up ... the beatings from Dad ... we're never going to be normal, Nicholas,' I explained with absolute belief in my words.

'Rebecca accepted me for who I am. Now I've lost her I realise just how much I need her,' he murmured, looking at me as if imploring me to believe him.

'Did she know about our past? About Dad? About your suicide attempt?' I asked, feeling like a complete shit for going down this line with him, but Nicholas needed to understand how things stood, he was damaged, just as I was, relationships for us would never work out in the long run.

'No, she didn't. But she was so fucking amazing, she would have understood. I've never felt trust like that before, Nathan. I think I fucking love her and now she never wants to see me again.'

My eyes widened. Love? Holy shit, this was so much more intense than I had expected. But love? Could we love? My broken brother and I? After everything we'd been through at the hands of our own supposed loved ones? My eyes narrowed as I thought about my relationship with Stella. Would it ever move beyond a physical need for me? Wincing as I thought back guiltily to her hurt expression as she left I wondered if it already had, but dismissed the ridiculous idea with a scowl.

'You know I respect you more than anyone in the world, Nathan, but I think you're wrong on this one, and I think I was a fool to follow your advice,' Nicholas said, laying himself down on the sofa and covering his eyes with a bent arm.

Shaking my head, I narrowed my eyes as Stella's face refused to fade from my mind. Fuck. Was I wrong? Was it possible that we could love and need someone as he was suggesting?

No, *no*. I didn't think I was wrong, and I was fairly sure that, given time, Nicholas would understand too and see that I was correct. Even with my conviction in this belief, I couldn't seem to erase the hurt look Stella had given me as she'd left, which wasn't helping my head to clear at all. I wasn't used to these feelings that seemed suddenly lodged in my chest, but it probably came pretty close to what normal people would describe as affection. Screwing my eyes shut I tried to shake it off, but only succeeded in making the bruise on my head throb. Fuck. Now not only did I have to try and sort out my brother's mess, I also had to deal with the very real possibility that just as I was developing a meaningful relationship for the first time in my life I'd probably pissed Stella off so much that I might never see her again, a thought that actually made my stomach churn with anxiety. Christ, what the hell was I doing advising my brother on relationships when I was clearly no better off? This whole night had been totally screwed up. But as I sat staring at my distraught brother whilst simultaneously panicking that Stella was gone for good I rephrased my last thought – it wasn't the night that was screwed up, it was *me*.

Thank you for reading! If you enjoyed this book please review on Amazon to help spread the word!

If you are keen to find out if Nathan and Stella can overcome their issues and continue their passionate relationship then the story continues in *Into The Light*, Book Three of The Untwisted Series, out soon!

I write for my readers, so I'd love to hear your thoughts, feel free get in touch with me:
E-mail: aliceraineauthor@gmail.com
Twitter: @AliceRaine1
Facebook: www.facebook.com/alice.raineauthor
Website: www.aliceraineauthor.com

When I write about my characters and scenes, I have certain images in my head. I've created a Pinterest page with these images in case you are curious. I hope you enjoy this little glimpse into Nicholas and Nathan's world. You can find it at http://www.pinterest.com/alice3083/

You will also find some teaser pics for upcoming books to whet your appetite!

Alice xx

The story continues in

Into the Light

The Untwisted Series #3

Into the Light, the third novel in the highly addictive Untwisted series follows on with the complex and intensely erotic relationship between the dark and domineering Nathaniel Jackson and timid Stella Marsden.

Passion runs wild as Nathan and Stella continue their illicit 'no-strings attached' meet-ups, but as Stella begins to fall for Nathan, his jealous side rears its ugly head. After a misunderstanding threatens to end their relationship once and for all, can Nathan move past the engrained behaviours of his past and learn to trust Stella, the only woman to ever tempt him to consider a 'real' relationship?

Enlightened

The Untwisted Series #4

Passionate, intense, and formidable, the Jackson brothers return in the deeply erotic final instalment of The Untwisted series. Nicholas and Rebecca are together and stronger than ever as they prepare for their upcoming wedding, but a series of misunderstandings threatens to ruin their big day – and possibly the foundation of their entire relationship. Meanwhile, Nathan and Stella are drawn into complications as Stella hides a secret from the man she loves that could tear them apart forever.

Can Nicholas and Nathan ever truly escape their dark past and find the happiness they thought would always be out of reach?

Christmas with Nicholas

An Untwisted Short Story

From the best-selling author of the Untwisted series comes a sexy seasonal short story.

Devilishly dark Nicholas Jackson is sexy, intense, and domineering but since meeting timid bookshop owner Rebecca, he discovers his softer side. Determined to give Rebecca the best Christmas of her life, Nicholas sets out to find the perfect gift. Only problem – he has absolutely no idea what to get her!

Can Nicholas give Rebecca a Christmas she'll never forget?